"Why don't you tell me the truth?"

Brooke started. "I am telling you the truth."

"Not all of it," Victor said. "I can see in your face there's something you don't want me to know."

"I thought you were a heart surgeon, not a psychiatrist."

He laughed. "Good research on your part, but I'm also pretty skilled at reading faces." Truth was, he did not understand why he had the feeling he knew her. He kept his voice low and soft, but he could see she caught the intensity anyway. "So go ahead and tell me. You want to find the painting because it belongs to your father. What's the other reason that brought you here?"

She took a deep breath and straightened, looking somehow more vulnerable. Vulnerable, small and scared. "I came to you because I believe you are the only person who can help me find that painting. And..."

"And what? Let's have it, Ms. Ramsey."

"And I think someone is..."

"Is what?"

Her voice dropped, so he had to lean closer to hear.

"Following me."

Books by Dana Mentink

Love Inspired Suspense

Killer Cargo
Flashover
Race to Rescue
Endless Night
Betrayal in the Badlands
Turbulence
Buried Truth
Escape from the Badlands
*Lost Legacy

*Treasure Seekers

DANA MENTINK

lives in California, where the weather is golden and the cheese is divine. Her family includes two girls (affectionately nicknamed Yogi and Boo Boo). Papa Bear works for the fire department; he met Dana doing a dinner theater production of *The Velveteen Rabbit*. Ironically, their parts were husband and wife.

Dana is a 2009 American Christian Fiction Writers Book of the Year finalist for romantic suspense and an award winner in the Pacific Northwest Writers Literary Contest. Her novel *Betrayal in the Badlands* won a 2010 *RT Book Reviews* Reviewer's Choice Award. She has enjoyed writing a mystery series for Barbour Books and more than ten novels to date for Harlequin's Love Inspired Suspense line.

She spent her college years competing in speech and debate tournaments all around the country. Besides writing, she busies herself teaching elementary school and reviewing books for her blog. Mostly, she loves to be home with her family, including a dog with social anxiety problems, a chubby box turtle and a quirky parakeet.

Dana loves to hear from her readers via her website at www.danamentink.com.

LOST LEGACY

DANA MENTINK

Love Inspired

Recycling programs
for this product may
not exist in your area.

LOVE INSPIRED BOOKS

ISBN-13: 978-0-373-67509-8

LOST LEGACY

Copyright © 2012 by Dana Mentink

This edition published by arrangement with Love Inspired Books.

® and TM are trademarks of Love Inspired Books, used under license. Trademarks indicated with ® are registered in the United States Patent and Trademark Office, the Canadian Trade Marks Office and in other countries.

www.LoveInspiredBooks.com

Printed in U.S.A.

Guard, through the Holy Spirit who dwells in us,
the treasure which has been entrusted to you.
—*2 Timothy* 1:14

To my faithful readers who have come along with me for this Treasure Seekers series. You inspire me to make each book better than the last.

right now. She's a computer genius among other things," Victor said. "My brother, Luca, is also a partner in this firm, but he's traveling at the moment."

Brooke eyed the two of them. "I can see the resemblance."

"Working with big brothers can have advantages and disadvantages," Stephanie said, with a wry look at Victor. "Have you got siblings, Ms. Ramsey?"

"Just a brother but he's…away."

Stephanie gave Brooke a friendly nod before turning to Victor. "Luca is going to be tied up for another two days." Her gaze flicked to Brooke and back again. "He said not to get into any messes while he's gone, but I think he might have meant that more for me than you."

Victor laughed. "Ms. Ramsey was just telling me that she needs access to Bayside College, but she hasn't told me why."

Brooke breathed deeply before she answered. "There is a tunnel system under the college. It's been there since the place was built in the 1930s. I have reason to believe there's a treasure hidden there, which I need to recover quickly."

He leaned forward. "Let's stop dancing around the issue, Ms. Ramsey. What's the treasure?"

She raised her chin a fraction. "A painting that belongs to my father."

"What kind of painting?"

She stared at him, and he could see her weighing whether or not to trust him. "It's a Tarkenton."

He didn't answer for a moment. "A Tarkenton? As in a work by L. Tarkenton?"

She nodded.

Considering he'd recently read about a Tarkenton fetching twenty million dollars at auction, it would be a treasure indeed. "How did your father wind up with it?"

Her eyes flicked away from his. "That's not important. The point is, I know where it is."

He considered, pulse quickening at the enticing possibility. She could be wrong. Barring that, her father could have obtained the painting illegally. The possibility that a work of art was tucked in the tunnels under Bayside College was beyond far-fetched. "That's certainly quite a prize, but we don't work for the payoff. We're all well established. I think you need an art historian, not the three of us. We couldn't authenticate it, even if we found the piece."

"I am an art historian, unofficially anyway. Look, I know you're not in it for the payoff and neither am I. The painting belongs to my father and he's…" She swallowed. "Never mind the details. My father had it sent to a professor at the college for examination, a man named Leo Colda, and it disappeared while in his possession."

Stephanie cocked her head. "Hang on. This rings a bell. Colda disappeared, too, didn't he?"

Brooke nodded. "He was last seen exiting the steam tunnels a month ago. I need to recover the painting. Time is running out. They're closing down

ONE

Victor Gage saw beneath the determined expression that Brooke Ramsey was hiding something. Although her red hair and splash of freckles lent her an impish quality, she was deadly serious at the moment.

She lifted her chin, her hands clasped together tightly. "Dr. Gage…"

"Please call me Victor. I haven't been a practicing surgeon for four years." He still felt the familiar twinge when he said it out loud. Though he smiled gently at her, she did not respond. Something about her seemed familiar.

Her words were measured and calm, but there was a strong current of emotion throbbing underneath. "I want to hire you to find a treasure."

He raised an eyebrow. "Why me?"

She glanced around the richly appointed office. "Because Treasure Seekers is your agency." She crossed her legs, long and lean, a dancer's body. "You've found things for people before. Yours is the only business in California that does this kind of work, I've heard."

"True, but we're not really a public agency. We are very selective. The cases we've taken on were strictly through private recommendation. Friends of friends generally. I'm surprised you've even heard about us."

"You found that Vermeer six months ago. You're the only one who can help us," she said.

For Victor the thrill came in unearthing the treasure, not the publicity that inevitably followed, but the Vermeer had made international headlines in spite of his refusal to be interviewed. "Us?"

"Me. I meant me."

He cocked his head. "There are plenty of good detective agencies you could go with. Why am I the only one?"

She shifted in the chair. "You have connections to Bayside College. Your family funded some buildings there."

He hid his surprise. She'd done some homework, just as he would have before a meeting like this. "My father did, yes."

She leaned forward. "Then they'll allow you access."

"To what?"

Stephanie Gage slipped into the room and joined them. Victor introduced his sister. He watched Brooke's reaction to Stephanie's frank stare. Brooke's gaze lingered on the scar that crossed his sister's cheekbone. "Stephanie is working on another case the college next term for a massive remodel and if I don't find the painting soon it will be destroyed." She bit her lip and looked at her lap.

He watched her cheeks flush, the curse of a fair, freckle-faced redhead. He got the impression there was something much more than treasure at stake. After giving her a moment to recover herself, he asked, "Why don't you tell me the truth?"

She started. "I am telling you the truth."

"Not all of it. I can see in your face there's something you don't want me to know."

"I thought you were a heart surgeon, not a psychiatrist."

He laughed. "Good research on your part, but I'm also pretty skilled at reading faces." Truth was, he did not understand why he was so intrigued by this particular face, why he had the feeling he knew her. He kept his voice low and soft, but he could see she caught the intensity anyway. "So go ahead and tell me. You want to find the painting because it belongs to your father. What's the other reason that brought you here?"

She took a deep breath and straightened, looking somehow more vulnerable since she'd taken off her jacket. Vulnerable, small and scared. "I came to you because I believe you are the only people who can help me find that painting. And…"

"And what? Let's have it, Ms. Ramsey."

"And I think someone is…"

"Is what?"

Her voice dropped so he had to lean closer to hear. "Following me."

Stephanie and Victor stared at Brooke, and she could feel her cheeks flame with embarrassment.

Victor's look was half suspicious, half amazed. He thought she was paranoid and, from the guarded expression on his sister's face, she agreed with him. Brooke was beginning to think it herself.

She waited in the outer office while they discussed the situation, even though she knew what the outcome would be. She thought about her brother. Tad's goofy smile played in her memory.

Chin up, he would remind her at every opportunity. Deep down he was a gentle soul, sweet and loving, and no one would ever convince her otherwise. She raised her head. She would find the Tarkenton and they'd have enough, more than enough to take care of Tad, to bring him home where he belonged. The door opened and she shot to her feet.

They emerged, their demeanor kind, professional and firm.

"I'm sorry, Ms. Ramsey," Stephanie said. Brooke was afraid to look her in the eye, so she focused on the second tiny gold hoop in Stephanie's ear, just above the lobe.

"We have several projects in progress right now and we don't feel we can give your case the attention it deserves."

Victor thanked her for coming and offered to help her find a private investigator. She declined.

As Brooke exited the outer office and headed for the elevator, she puzzled it over. Of course a successful doctor, already wealthy, who found treasures on a lark wouldn't be interested in her fanciful tale of a vanished Tarkenton painting. And he and his sister would definitely be put off by some paranoid woman who believed someone was following her.

As she waited for the elevator, the fright she'd experienced over the past few months seemed ridiculous. The lady she'd thought was tailing her, the phone calls. She swallowed. Was her mind going? Was it an early manifestation of the disease that was eating away at her father? A version of the terrible genetic error visited on Tad?

She shook it off and willed the elevator to hurry. The quiet of the hallway was oppressive. Didn't anyone else work on this floor of the San Francisco building? She longed to get home to Southern California where the fog did not lie like an oppressive blanket over the spring sunshine. Shivering, she realized with a start that she'd left her jacket in Gage's office.

She would rather lose it than go back and face the former doctor who already thought she was delusional. It had taken every ounce of courage to seek him out. She had not one bit of bravery left. A familiar sense of failure hung heavy on her shoulders. The elevator doors slid open and Brooke stepped forward until she saw the lady in the back, her hair a perfect black in spite of the fifty years or so written on her hardened face.

That face.

That woman.

Brooke knew her; she'd seen her back home at the coffee shop, at the library.

Fear bubbled up inside and she backed away.

The woman stepped forward, a question in her eyes. She reached into a black slouch bag.

Brooke didn't wait. She whirled around and ran toward the end of the corridor, slamming through the stairwell door. Her feet moved faster than she'd thought possible as she plunged down three flights of stairs, heart thundering.

She did not know exactly why, but the woman had been stalking her, waiting to make her move. The cement corridor echoed her frantic run as she pelted down the stairs.

Get to the next floor. There will be people around. She can't hurt you with people around.

Brooke continued on her flight until she saw the door marked Floor Six just ahead. Only a half-dozen steps left to go when she heard the unmistakable sound. The door began to open.

For all his years as a surgeon and the personal trauma he'd survived, Victor thought he was immune to surprise, but he found himself taken aback at Brooke Ramsey's declaration that someone was following her. They'd exchanged a few words. She'd shaken his hand, her fingers cold and small in his grip, and practically run out the door, before he could even recommend someone else to help her. He was grateful for the chance to try to sort out his tangle of feelings as he returned to his desk and sank into the chair.

"What are you thinking?" Stephanie said, her hand on his shoulder.

"Me? Just wondering if we did the right thing refusing her case."

"If she's telling the truth, she needs the cops, not us. If she's not..."

"Then she's crazy?"

Stephanie sighed. "I've wondered that about myself many a time."

He wanted to take her hand and squeeze it, to tell her that there were brighter days ahead, but he didn't think he could sound convincing and she wouldn't welcome the gesture anyway. He felt certain that all his brighter days were firmly in the past. Long gone, like his wife, Jennifer. He looked at the framed picture on his desk of a smiling Jen with her arms around him. Ironic that the afternoon she died she was wearing the same colorful scarf she'd been sporting the day he'd proposed.

Jen was gone; the joyful years were now buried deep and sealed over like an ugly, improperly healed wound. Now the only thing left was Treasure Seekers. It was the single reason he pulled himself out of bed some mornings. There were treasures still to be found in the world, the perfect job for his mixture of tenacity and curiosity. "Something about Ms. Ramsey is familiar. Why do I feel like I've seen her somewhere?"

Stephanie headed for the door. He recognized the determination in her perfect posture. "I'll go do a little digging and get back to you."

Victor stared after her. He replayed his last question to Brooke Ramsey in his mind, after he'd refused her case.

"What will you do now?" Why had he even said that? Why did he have the desire to keep her from leaving?

She'd turned her head, the light catching the determination in her profile and the streak of little-girl vulnerability. "I'm going to find another way to return my father's painting. Thank you for your time." Then she'd bolted out the door.

His eyes wandered back to the chair where she'd sat, looking at him with emotions that went far deeper than her words. It took him a moment to realize she'd left her jacket on the chair. He fingered the soft brown suede, remembering how it accentuated the almost luminous quality of her coppery hair. A light citrusy scent clung to the material.

He hurried to the door, calling to his secretary. "Trudy, I'm going to step out for a minute."

She nodded. "I've got a message for Ms. Ramsey. Did you get her cell phone number?"

"Yes," he said, frowning. "A message from whom?"

"Her sister, asking for a return call."

Just a brother, she'd said.

Without a word, he took off running toward the elevators.

Brooke froze, heart slamming into her ribs, paralyzed. Should she run by the door or back up the stairs?

She was about to bolt past when the door swung open. A startled maintenance worker jerked when he saw her.

"Man, you scared me," he said.

"Sorry," she managed after sucking in a breath. "Is… Did you see anyone out there? A lady with black hair and a big bag?"

He chewed a piece of gum and considered. "Saw someone like that earlier in the lobby. She looked around for a while and made a phone call, then I lost track of her."

She nodded her thanks and continued on down until she reached the lobby. Opening the door and peeking out, she was relieved to see no sign of the lady. Trying to appear calm even though her heart was still thundering inside her, she walked to the reception desk and asked the attendant to summon her a taxi. While she waited, her attention divided between looking out the glass doors for the taxi in the bustle of the financial district and watching the elevator and stairwell for any sign of her stalker, Brooke shivered.

Could be the lady was completely innocent, but Brooke was positive it was the same person she'd noticed the week before in San Diego, watching her from a parked car.

Brooke positioned herself nearer to the glass doors where she would be easily seen by passersby and the front desk person. Once again she was overreacting. Her fears were silly. She tried to focus her thoughts on the next step. Since Victor had declined, she had to find another way to get access to the tunnels under the college. How? Dean Lock would never allow it, not considering his hatred of her father. The police wouldn't get involved. Who could pressure the dean into allowing her access?

No one but Victor Gage.

She pushed the dark thought aside.

God will help me through this, she thought. He'd held on to her and her father and brother through a lifetime of struggle. He wouldn't turn His back on them now. She didn't need anyone's help anyway.

The elevator doors opened. Brooke was startled to see Victor step out, troubled eyes scanning the room until he found hers. There was an intensity in his face she hadn't seen before.

He'd changed his mind. Her heart leaped until she saw her jacket in his hand. Merely returning a forgotten item. Disappointment swirled inside, but she held up her chin and plastered a gracious smile on her face.

A moment later the smile fell away. Brooke watched over Victor's shoulder as the black-haired woman emerged from the stairwell, her expression grim.

Brooke gasped and took a step backward.

In a fog of confusion, she saw a look of horror twist Victor's handsome features, his eyes rounding over her shoulder as he looked out the glass doors.

She had no idea what had startled him until the glass shattered around them and Victor pulled her to the floor.

TWO

Victor saw the situation unfold, but his head did not believe it. One moment he was heading toward Brooke Ramsey, wondering at the frightened look on her face. The next, he saw a car pull up outside the office, the window rolled down just far enough for him to see a gun thrust through the opening. He had a split second to leap on top of Brooke and carry her to the ground before three shots drilled through the glass. They tumbled along the tile floor, small pieces of the safety glass crackling underneath them. There was a scream from somewhere as the car pulled away and out of sight.

Her breath came in short pants against his cheek. He pushed away a section of her glossy hair and looked into her eyes, so close he could see his own expression mirrored there.

"Are you hurt?"

She tried a few times to answer before any words came out. "I don't think so. What happened?"

He took another look to make sure the car hadn't

returned before he rolled off her and moved her away from the glass. "A shooter," he managed, before he noticed the front desk person sprinting across the lobby, shouting into a radio.

Victor followed his progress. Brooke must have, too, because he heard her gasp, her hands flying to her mouth. Then his body was moving on instinct, feet crunching over the broken glass, mind running like a mad thing as he raced to the dark-haired woman lying motionless on the floor.

Mid-fifties, he guessed as he checked her vitals. No breathing, no heartbeat, bullet wound visible on her forehead. He knew the prognosis of a bullet plowing through the frontal lobe of the brain, but he ignored it, tilting her jaw to open the airway and starting chest compressions. Every few cycles he rechecked the vitals without much hope.

Cold horror seeped into him as he was transported back to the moment when he'd awakened in a wrecked car, Jennifer unconscious and broken next to him. He could still feel the warmth of her body under his hands as he frantically tried to restart her heart. There must have been people there, too, as there were now, standing helplessly, dialing cell phones, calling encouragement to the victims of the awful accident, but he hadn't heard them. Everything faded into a mumbling haze except the reality of his hands on her ribs, his lips blowing air into her mouth, the fading pulse under his frantic fingertips.

"Help me, God," he'd said, because that's what Jen would have prayed.

And He hadn't.

And Victor couldn't either.

Jennifer was gone.

Victor knew with the same sickening certainty that the black-haired woman was gone, too. He could force her heart to pump, squeeze it into pushing the blood around, but the life, that indefinable force that separates the living from the dead, was gone. He continued the compressions anyway, shoulders burning, until the paramedics arrived and took over the effort. When he finally did move away, he saw Brooke staring at him in shock. An officer took her by the arm and another one escorted him to a nearby hallway, away from the broken glass and the death that lay in awkward display on the cold tile floor.

He was surprised to find that his hands were shaking, so he stuffed them into his pockets as the officer began to ask him questions. He retold the strange interview with Brooke and her assertion that someone was following her. With a start, Victor remembered why he'd gone to the lobby in the first place.

"Someone called my office looking for Ms. Ramsey, pretending to be her sister."

The officer raised an eyebrow and dutifully recorded the information. "Why don't you sit down here while we look into some things, Mr. Gage?" The officer moved off and Victor caught sight of

Brooke talking to another cop, the freckles standing out strikingly against the paleness of her skin.

He wished he could settle on one feeling, but a stream of conflicting emotions surged through him. Post-traumatic shock, he figured. He'd just witnessed a murder, and if he hadn't been there it would have been Brooke on the floor. The thought sickened him.

Stephanie appeared, eyes wide and scared. She took hold of his arms, squeezing hard. "Are you all right?"

He reassured her, bringing her briefly up to speed. Stephanie shook her head. "Drive-by shooting? Gang related, maybe?"

He shrugged, and he read in her face that she didn't believe it was a random shooting any more than he did. He glanced over at Brooke.

Brooke nodded at some question from the officer and looked as though she might cry.

Was this related to the phone call? Or was this a random shooting? He should help her figure it out, dive into the situation with all the zeal he possessed, isolate the problem, cure the ailment.

He looked again at Brooke as the officer led her to a chair. "It was the woman…the woman I thought was following me back in San Diego."

The same woman?

She avoided looking at him.

It was just as well.

Brooke needed help, but he was not the man to give it to her, or to anyone else.

* * *

Brooke had to force herself to remain in the chair. She had the insane desire to run, to plow through the ruined front doors and sprint all the way back to San Diego to her father. She'd heard the front desk man say something about gangs and drive-by shootings but she knew in her soul, deep down in the instinctive part, that the bullet had been intended for her, not the black-haired lady who had been wheeled out on a stretcher to the waiting ambulance. She could tell by the expression on Victor's face when the medics arrived that the lady would not survive. Had the woman been trying to help her? To warn her? Of what? Of whom? Brooke's head spun.

After an hour of questioning, waiting and more questioning, she was spent. Blinking back tears, she pulled the phone out of her purse and dialed. It rang once, twice, until someone picked up.

"Dad," she breathed, trying to keep her voice steady.

A woman's voice answered. "Brooke, it's Denise. Your father's taking a nap. Are you okay? You sound funny."

Brooke relayed the events as simply as she could to her father's cousin.

Denise gasped into the phone. "What? Are you hurt? Who was shot?"

Brooke reassured her, "A lady I don't know was killed. I wasn't hurt, thanks to—" she shot a look at Victor, who had closed his eyes and leaned his head against the wall behind him "—the man I was meeting, to look into the situation. He kept me out of the line of fire."

"Brooke, this is crazy. You need to come home right now. Tell that man you don't care about the painting anymore and head home before something worse happens."

She sighed. "He didn't take the case anyway."

Denise exhaled loudly. "Then you've got no reason to stay. Come home where you'll be safe."

Brooke glanced at Victor, who was now gazing at her with haunted eyes. She wondered for a moment what it would be like to bring someone back from the brink of death. Or fail to. She blinked away the thoughts. "I'm going to stay the night, try to plead my case with Dean Lock myself."

"It's a lost cause. You know that. Way too much past history there."

"I know but I've got to try. How's…how's Dad?"

"It was a good day. He was very together. We finished up another chapter and he even remembered where he'd put some of the notes he took from our trip to Cambria."

Brooke smiled, remembering how excited her father had been, researching Tarkenton's time in Cambria. It was there, six months ago, that he had purchased the unsigned painting at an estate sale, a painting he was absolutely convinced was the work of Tarkenton. For months he'd been studying it, fussing over it, she thought uncomfortably. She sighed, wondering for a moment if it wouldn't have been better for him never to have discovered the thing. It seemed to be the root of the strange trouble she found herself in now.

But recalling the sheer joy on his face when he showed it to her, the clarity of his mind as he took her through each aspect of the painting, the application of color, the emotionally controlled realism, the perfect execution only possible from a master. She would not trade those moments for anything. She tuned back in.

"Brooke," Denise was saying, "your father would not want you to put yourself in danger to find out what happened to his painting. You're more valuable to him that any work of art."

"I know, and I'm just going to give it one more try and then I'm on my way home. Don't tell Dad about the shooting, please. It will just upset him."

"I don't like keeping things from your father. He's not a child, Brooke."

I know that, she wanted to snap. *He's my father, isn't he?* Instead she bit back the frustration. Donald Ramsey was not a child; he was a man of ferocious intellect and voracious curiosity, but more and more the genetic condition was turning him into someone she didn't know. Each day brought him deeper into that mental fog from which someday he would not be able to escape.

Denise was helping, too, keeping his mind active, engaging him in finishing his book, making sure he had contact with Tad. *Patience, Brooke.* "I understand. Maybe you could not mention it unless he asks about me." She paused. "Has he? Asked about me?"

She could sense Denise struggling with the truth. "Well...we've been really busy here, honey. We visited Tad today, and you know that's hard on your father."

Brooke blinked hard at a sudden wash of tears. *It's hard on everyone.* "No problem. I'll call you soon."

She hung up before the emotion got the best of her. Phone gripped in her hand, she tried to take some calming breaths.

Gotta help Dad. Gotta make things right. Time is running out.

Victor's voice made her jump.

"Are you okay?"

There was sympathy in his face, probably the kind he gave to any crazy person he came across. "Yes. Okay. Thank you for...what you did."

He didn't respond, just looked at her with those piercing green-gold eyes until she couldn't stand it anymore. She walked to the nearest officer, feeling as though she'd been in that lobby for a lifetime instead of an hour and a half. "Can I go now?"

He asked her a few more questions, got her cell phone number and the name of her hotel and offered to call her a taxi.

"I'll drive her."

Brooke was startled to find Victor standing at her elbow. "I can take a taxi."

"My car is around back."

Stephanie walked over. "Stay here," she said to Victor. "We've got some things to look into."

"No, Steph. I'll be back soon. I need to take Brooke to her hotel."

Stephanie looked unhappy, but she did not attempt to persuade her brother. "Okay. I'll be waiting for you." She paused a moment next to Brooke. Her eyes were guarded, but Brooke could see concern buried deep down. "I'm sorry this happened, Ms. Ramsey. Be careful."

Brooke felt suddenly exhausted. She only wanted to get to her hotel room, sink into a hot bath and forget the past few hours. Maybe if she tried really hard, she could convince herself it was all a dream, a very bad dream. "Thank you."

Victor led the way to the parking lot, where he opened the door to a spotlessly clean Mercedes. She leaned her head back on the leather seat and closed her eyes as Victor eased them through the crush of the San Francisco financial district, suited men and women, bicycle messengers and the constant supply of taxis weaving through the lanes. He didn't say a word, and that was just fine with her. The sun was low in the sky now, outlining the tall buildings in harsh shadow.

She shot a peek at his profile, dark hair cut short on the sides, bangs long enough to show the slightest tendency to curl. Thick brows and a strong chin that sported the shadow of the beard that would no doubt emerge if he wasn't impeccably shaved.

"I overheard you talking on the phone to your mother."

Brooke stiffened. "My mom is gone. That was my father's cousin. My unofficial aunt."

"Is your father ill?"

The question might have been rude if it hadn't resonated with a certain compassion. Or was it clinical curiosity? She sighed. "Yes, he's...he's not well."

"And you're trying to find the painting because you think time is running out for him?"

She shoved her hands under her thighs. "Isn't that kind of a personal question after you washed your hands of my case?"

A ghost of a smile danced on his lips. "You're right. Poor bedside manner. I apologize."

"Why aren't you a doctor anymore?" she blurted out, aghast at her own forwardness. What had come over her?

He didn't look at her, but she saw his grip tighten on the steering wheel. "I needed a break."

"So you went from being a doctor to a treasure hunter?"

He offered a small smile. "Luca's idea. He's always been part Indiana Jones."

She brightened. "Do you think *he* would take my case, then?"

Victor laughed. "We usually stick together on

these decisions. Treasure Seekers is really important to all of us."

"Indiana Jones would have done it." They exchanged a look and both of them laughed until Brooke flopped her head back against the seat. "Well, you did save my life, so I guess I can forgive you for turning me down."

"I'm glad," he said.

"I think I've heard your name before somewhere. Are you an art aficionado?"

"No, but my wife was." He cleared his throat. "I took up treasure hunting after she was killed."

Brooke felt herself flush. "I'm sorry."

He nodded, not looking at her. "Me, too."

They pulled up at the hotel and Brooke got out quickly, hoping Victor wouldn't offer to walk her in. He did anyway, in spite of her protests. Something about him made her stomach flutter.

The hotel carpet was plush, the lobby tasteful with graceful indoor trees and richly upholstered chairs arranged in cozy groups. It all looked so normal, so unbelievably calm compared to the anxiety storming inside her.

He walked with her to the elevator and they got inside, the silence thickening between them. Brooke could not figure out what to think about the man next to her. She wanted to be angry with him for brushing her off, but those feelings were outweighed by his heroic effort in the lobby and the shadow in his eyes when he spoke of his wife.

She would have shaken her head to ward off the thoughts if he wasn't standing so close, close enough for her to catch the faint musky aftershave and see the tiny cut on his cheek, no doubt caused by his dive into the glass.

A big man wearing dark glasses got into the elevator. She jumped as he dropped the clipboard he was carrying, which fell to the floor with a sharp crack. Victor gave her a reassuring look as the man apologized, and she offered him a shaky smile.

Victor saw her up to the fifth floor and waited until she slid her key card and opened the door. She turned to thank him again.

He held up a hand to stop her. "I hope you find what you're looking for."

He'd turned and walked away before she could answer.

I hope you do, too.

Brooke closed the door with a deep sigh and leaned her forehead against the cool panel before she turned around to find a man standing next to the bed.

THREE

Victor checked his iPhone.

Message from his brother.

Steph told me what happened. Don't take that case. You're not getting the whole story.

Victor could picture his little brother's determined face. He'd seen Luca's same ferocious resolve to help after Jen died. It was the reason, he suspected, his brother had come up with the Treasure Seekers idea in the first place, a way for Luca to exercise his own constant need for adventure and give his big brother a purpose again.

Four years later, it had only partially worked.

Yes, it had kept his mind busy, passionately absorbed in the next prize waiting to be found, but it had not healed his heart. That was still a lump of cold lead, untouchable and numb.

He was about to dial his brother's number when he heard Brooke scream.

He bolted back to her room just as she tore open

the door and hurtled out into his arms, nearly knocking him down.

Eyes wide with terror, she gasped, "There's someone in my room."

He guided her behind him. "Stay here."

In spite of his order, he felt her hand on his back as he eased the door open. She edged in behind him as he slowly pushed the door wider.

The man with close-cropped silver hair and a face that spoke of hard living sat on the bed, arms folded. He showed no sign of agitation at being discovered.

"What are you doing here?" Victor said. Brooke stepped up to get a closer look, one hand still resting on Victor's back.

The man looked closely at both of them with expressionless blue eyes before he answered. "Hello, Doc."

Brooke jerked, eyes shifting from Victor to the man on the bed. "You know each other?"

"Yes." Tuney stood. "Dr. Gage hired me to do some investigation for him four years ago. How are you, Ms. Ramsey?"

"Who are you?" Brooke said warily.

"A detective. I'm working on a case that started with a theft at a certain museum."

Brooke sagged and went to the nearest chair, dropping heavily onto the upholstered seat.

Victor eyed Tuney carefully, the muscles in his stomach knotted. "Why are you following her?"

Brooke gazed at the carpet as she spoke. "I recognize him now. You came to my house and asked all kinds of questions after the robbery, didn't you, Mr. Tuney?" When she lifted her head, he noticed the smudges under her eyes and the fatigue that seemed to permeate her body. "Four years ago my father was the assistant curator at the Museum of Culture here in San Francisco. There was a theft—three pieces were stolen from the delivery truck just outside the museum." She shot a harsh look at Tuney. "My father had nothing to do with it. He tried to call for help once he realized what was happening, but it was too late."

"That's one version," Tuney said. "Another is your father leaked the information to someone who arranged for the theft. That's why he lost his job, isn't it?"

Anger flared in Brooke's face. "He lost his job because the museum needed a scapegoat, and Jeffrey Lock, the head curator, made sure my father took the fall."

The disbelief on Tuney's face was clear along with an inexplicable current of anger. "Lock lost his job, too. That's why he works at Bayside now. The art was probably sold on the black market, and someone made a fortune. Any idea who?"

"It wasn't the Ramsey family," Brooke snapped. "We're not exactly swimming in money, in case you haven't noticed. We left San Francisco because we couldn't afford to stay here anymore after the incident. My father owns a fifteen-year-old car and a run-down house in San Diego."

"Sometimes art freaks steal for the sake of owning what they can't buy. And the thing about art freaks is, they constantly need to collect more and more. It's a sickness, see. So why are you using the name Ramsey? Your father's name is Andrews, isn't it?"

She slumped. "He forced us to use my mother's maiden name. Too many people hate us now."

Victor felt his stomach shrink. Brooke Ramsey, formerly Brooke Andrews, daughter of Donald Andrews, the one man he abhorred more than any other person on the planet.

Tuney raised an eyebrow. "I understand your father is now in possession of a painting that might be a Tarkenton."

Brooke gaped. "How did you know that?"

Tuney shrugged, his mouth drawn, eyes flashing. "Your father contacted Professor Colda at the university. Funny thing. Professor Colda went missing, shortly after. Found a note in his office. An address. Guess whose?"

Brooke shrugged in exasperation. "Ours, no doubt. That makes sense, since my father sent him the painting to appraise."

"Yes, your father contacted Colda and then the guy disappeared. Could be your father and the good professor had a falling out? Maybe the learned professor started to ask questions about how your father acquired the Tarkenton? Reasonable, since Dad already has a black mark on his reputation. Maybe he had to make Colda disappear."

Brooke lifted her chin and Victor thought he saw her lips tremble before she glared at Tuney. "In spite of the news reports, my father's character is impeccable. Can you say the same for yours?"

Victor collected himself and corralled his shock. "Mr. Tuney, none of this gives you the right to break into her room."

"I didn't break in. Gave the maid a happy story that I was her father looking to surprise his daughter." His lips quirked. "Besides, you didn't mind my methods when I was working for you."

Brooke stood. "You hired him?"

Victor shook his head. "Not this time. Four years ago, after the robbery."

Brooke was pacing the floor now, strides long and graceful, her cheeks flushed. "Because of what happened at the museum? Why would you care about that? What's your interest in the theft?"

"I have no interest whatsoever," Victor said, voice low.

"I don't understand," she said.

"One thing I've learned in this business. If something smells fishy, it usually is," Tuney said. "I've got a personal reason to be involved."

"Who are you working for now?" Victor said, turning back to Tuney.

Tuney shrugged. "That's not your concern."

Brooke crossed her arms. "Whatever you two

think you know about my father is wrong. He's a good man. He didn't steal anything back then and he hasn't stolen anything now."

"So why are you here in San Francisco?" Tuney said, jerking a thumb at Victor. "Talking to him? Going to do a little treasure hunting?"

Victor held up a hand. "I don't think that's any of your business, Mr. Tuney. The lady can talk with whomever she wants."

"Oh, I think it's my business, all right."

"How's that?"

"One thing you should both know. I'm a busy man, so sometimes I hire people to do freelancing for me. In this case, I had someone keeping tabs on you in San Diego and on your trip up here."

Victor felt a tingle of unease in his spine. "Who?"

"Gal by the name of Fran." He looked at Brooke, a flash of emotion crossing his face. "I was scheduled to meet her but things didn't work out. Maybe you saw her."

"Saw her?" Brooke echoed.

"Yeah," Tuney said, his eyes shifting from hers to Victor's. His voice trembled slightly, and he cleared his throat. "She was shot in your lobby a few hours ago."

The walls seemed to blur before Brooke's eyes. She staggered back and felt Victor's arm around her waist, steadying her, before she pulled away. "The black-haired woman worked for you?"

"Yes. Off the books, of course. She's the one who found your father's address in Colda's office, so she started tailing you. Followed you to San Francisco, to Gage's office building. I went to meet her. Got there just in time to join the crowd of bystanders who collected after the shooting." He cleared his throat again. "It was clear she wasn't going to make it, even with Dr. Gage's help, so I decided to come to meet with you personally."

"Did you tell all this to the police?" Victor asked.

Tuney's eyes narrowed. "Not yet. I figured I would fill them in right after I talked to you."

Words failed Brooke. All she could think about was the lady lying on the lobby floor with the life ebbing out of her.

"Brooke's going back home soon, so there's no reason for you to continue to pursue her."

"I want the truth. That's what I get paid to find out, and now, since Fran's been killed, I have even more reason to stay on this. She was a good woman and whoever is responsible needs to be punished." Tuney moved toward Brooke but Victor stepped in between them. Tuney continued, "Get me some time with your father, Brooke. He can come clean, admit to his part in the robbery and cop to whatever he did to Colda and had done to Fran. He's a sick man, I understand. He'll want to do the right thing before it's too late."

"Stop it," Brooke screamed, tears pooling in her eyes. "My father is okay. He's okay."

"Leave her alone." Victor drew himself up to his full six feet three. Tuney did not miss the gesture and eased back.

"Or your aunt Denise could talk to me," Tuney said thoughtfully. "She might have some info that would put the incident to rest."

Brooke didn't even ask how Tuney managed to know all the intimate details of her family's life. "You're wrong about everything."

He shrugged. "You should make it easy on your father. Get him to talk to me."

"What if she doesn't?" Victor said, voice low.

"Then I stick to Ms. Ramsey like the proverbial glue."

"You're no better than a stalker," Victor snapped.

"I prefer to think of it as determination rather than stalking. Funny how you didn't mind my tactics when you wanted answers of your own."

Victor gestured to the door. "I think you'd better leave, Mr. Tuney."

Tuney hesitated, and Brooke hated the scornful look on his face.

"I'll go," he said, "but you'll be seeing me in your rearview mirror until this thing is solved and Fran's murderer is caught." He stopped as he got to the door. "One thing you might consider. Could be that shoot-

ing today was random, but it could also be that someone else is interested in your situation."

"No," Brooke mumbled, head whirling.

"Better to get it all out in the open before somebody else winds up dead."

"Get out," Victor snarled.

Tuney strode out the door, leaving them in silence.

Victor gestured for her to sit on the bed and he
took the chair. "We need to contact the police and
fill them in on everything Tuney said."

She tried for a steady tone. "First you need to tell
me what's going on. You know about the robbery and
you hired Tuney before. I'm not moving an inch until
you tell me the truth."

"The truth?" he said quietly. "That's all I've been
trying to find out for four years."

Pain surged through her. All the shame, all the humiliation. Her father had never really been able to put
it behind him, and now it was all going to be raked
up again. Her mind was still spinning from Tuney's
intrusion. "What is happening? It was just supposed
to be a meeting. Now there's been a shooting and this
detective shows up. How well do you know him?"

"I hired him to investigate the circumstances of
my wife's death. He wasn't able to solve the case, so
we parted ways."

Brooke felt a tremor inside, a deep foreboding
slithering through her body. "When…when was your
wife killed?"

His eyes bored into hers. "September fifth, four years ago."

"September fifth?" She gaped. "That's the day my—"

"Father's museum was robbed, I know."

She did not understand the expression on his face, a mixture of anguish and burning intensity. "There was an accident," she whispered. "A few blocks from the museum. I remember reading about it in the paper."

His voice was feverish, brow furrowed, and she could hear a deep current of emotion behind the words. "At three forty-five, September fifth, a man fleeing the scene of the robbery plowed into our car and killed my wife. The driver was never caught. I hired Tuney to find out who was involved in the robbery so I could nail the guy."

"You hired Tuney to investigate my father?"

"And anyone else who might have been involved."

She felt sick. "You think...you believe my father is the one? That he robbed his own museum and hired the man who killed your wife?"

"Tuney didn't find any proof."

"But that's what you believe...deep down...isn't it?"

After a moment, he reached for his phone. "I'm going to call Dean Lock and arrange a meeting for us, tomorrow, if possible."

"Us?" She looked at him, openmouthed. "You're taking my case?"

"No," he said as he dialed. "But I'm going to go with you to meet the dean."

"Why would you do that?"

He stared at her. "Do you believe in God, Brooke?"

She started at the abruptness of the question, his eyes burning into hers. "Without a doubt."

"Well, I don't. My wife did, but I always told her I would never let anyone or anything take charge of my destiny but me. I don't believe there's a God that guides us through our daily lives. I don't believe it for one moment, but there's something going on here that I can't explain. The day your life fell apart, mine did, too, and now, all these years later, you walk into my office."

"Coincidence. It's got to be. How could the robbery be connected to what's happening now?"

"I don't know, but here you are claiming another painting has been stolen from your father."

"It's not just a claim. It's the truth," she snapped.

"Maybe it has nothing to do with what happened four years ago, but I'm not going to let it go until I know for sure."

She stared at the granite expression on his face, feeling a wave of anguish wash over her. "I had no idea. I remember hearing that a woman was killed, but I was too wrapped up in what was happening to my father to pay much attention. I never would have come to you if I had... It has to be a crazy coincidence."

She saw something glittering in his eyes, something hard and unforgiving. A bank of fog rolled across the sun, sending dark shadows skittering across the room. "I don't believe in coincidences either," he said. "But I do believe that someone is going to pay for killing my wife."

"My father wasn't responsible," she whispered.

"Then the truth will set us all free, won't it?" he said.

FOUR

"Absolutely not," Dean Lock said, lacing his fingers together. One hand was stiff, swollen at the joints, like a withered tree branch. Behind him a set of windows looked out on a courtyard thick with shrubs and a series of wooden benches. The office they now sat in was tucked behind the outer reception area, painted a soothing ivory color, the desk a rich, dark wood. Victor's feet sank into the plush carpet.

He had the same trim, polished look that Victor remembered from seeing the man two years before. Victor's father had bestowed a generous endowment to the university at that time. Polished but tired, as if he'd traveled many miles since their last meeting. His brows were drawn together and the furrows on his forehead were pronounced. Victor felt rather than saw Brooke's body tense in the chair next to him.

"We just need to take a look, to satisfy Ms. Ramsey's curiosity," Victor said, keeping his voice light. "There was a police report of a student who witnessed Colda exiting the tunnels just before he disappeared."

"I'm well aware of that." Lock's expression was amused. "Colda was my employee. Based on that one report, you believe Colda stashed a supposedly invaluable painting down there for safekeeping? A Tarkenton?" His words dripped with incredulity.

Victor chuckled. "Stranger things have happened."

Lock nodded. "True, but a whim isn't a good enough reason to take on the liability. I'm sorry. The tunnels are in a state of disrepair. Dangerous, to say the least."

"The university won't be held liable," Victor said. "Ms. Ramsey and I will act at our own risk."

She nodded, the overhead light sparkling in her hair. He could see it was killing her to keep silent during the exchange.

Lock shook his head. "Your reason is too far-fetched to merit the risk. There have never been any undiscovered Tarkentons and there are certainly not any underneath this university."

Victor shrugged. "Far-fetched, but not impossible. Brooke says Donald Ramsey sent the painting here to Colda. Now both the painting and the professor are missing."

"The police have searched the tunnels. They found nothing out of place and no sign of any painting."

Brooke broke in, "Then it won't do any harm to check again."

Victor sighed inwardly, wishing she had stayed quiet. As he suspected, Lock took offense.

The dean's gray eyes narrowed. "Harm? I believe

your father has caused enough harm to me to last a lifetime."

He heard Brooke exhale slowly. "Dean Lock, my father did not engineer that theft at the museum. I am sorry that you lost your position as head curator there but—"

"But heads had to roll and mine was the one that did." His eyes narrowed. "Someone knew the delivery schedule for those paintings. It was clearly an inside job."

"So it could have been you," she answered quietly.

Victor was surprised at her courage to speak even though her lips were trembling.

Lock leaned back as if she'd struck him before he swiveled his eyes to Victor. "I'm disappointed to see you're throwing in with her. Four years ago you hired an investigator to find evidence that her father was guilty."

Brooke's face flushed, and Victor fought an unexpected urge to take her hand. "I hired Tuney to look at every suspect, and that included you."

The ghost of a smile played across his face as he massaged his bad hand. "You made your father angry doing that."

"It wasn't the first time. Your friendship with my father aside, I had to find proof of who might have caused my wife's death."

"But you didn't, because there wasn't anything to incriminate me. I loved that museum. Why would I engineer a robbery?"

Because you are an art freak. The chance to own a rare piece thrills you like nothing else on earth. Because, as my father said, you love dead artists far more than any living. "We're not here to imply anything."

"Good, because I had nothing to do with that robbery."

Victor held up a hand. "And Tuney found nothing to incriminate Donald either. Tuney's back, by the way. He's been following Brooke."

"Really? Who hired him?"

"He wouldn't say who hired him, but it can't be another coincidence."

The dean sighed, a long, mournful exhale that seemed to shrink him several inches. "Victor, I understand your need for closure on this." His eyes clouded. "I've lost people, too, a woman I loved more than anyone else in the world, as a matter of fact, but getting involved in this ridiculous treasure hunt is not going to bring Jennifer back."

"I know that," Victor barked, surprising himself with his tone. He continued more softly, "I've accepted the loss and dealt with the grief, but the thing I cannot make peace with is that nobody paid for the crime. If this situation is in any way connected to what happened four years ago like Tuney seems to believe, I need to know the truth, all of it."

Lock smiled and sat back in his chair. "Your father's nickname for you was right on the money."

Victor felt his cheeks flush and swiveled his eyes

away from Brooke. "So will you allow us to go in? I would take it as a personal favor. Besides, we might just find the treasure of a lifetime." Victor didn't want to go over Lock's head, knowing it would destroy his relationship with his father's old friend. He didn't want to, but if Lock proved an obstacle, Victor would circumvent the problem one way or another. He always did.

Dean Lock cocked his head. "All right. Because you are Wyatt's son and because I try to be a fair-minded man, I'll take you into the tunnels myself. You'll see that there's nothing there but rusted pipes and rats."

If Lock intended to frighten Brooke with the mention of rodents, it didn't seem to have any effect. She nodded solemnly. "Thank you, Dean Lock. I know you believe the worst about my father and I'm sorry to have to ask. I appreciate your help."

Victor sensed her humility. He could hear in the clipped syllables what it cost to speak the words. Situations reversed, he was not sure he would have said them. "When can we see it?"

To Victor's great surprise, the dean rose stiffly to his feet. "How about right now?"

While the dean went to retrieve his keys, Brooke paced around the office. "I can't believe he said yes."

Victor smiled. "Frankly, I can't either. I was prepared for more of a fight."

She laughed. "Thank you," she said, putting her

hand on his arm and feeling the hard strength there that made her fingertips tingle. "I truly appreciate it. You don't have to go with me. I'll pay you for your time."

He raised an eyebrow. "It's not a matter of money."

She saw the anger in his eyes, deep down, nestled like a live thing. Could he see the hurt in hers? she wondered. The grief that was kindled when her father was stripped of his job and his dignity? She moved away. "Of course. I understand. This isn't about the painting for you." His eyes followed her and she felt suddenly nervous. She began to prowl around, scanning the pictures on the wall. One caught her eye, a photo of a much younger Jeffrey Lock in a tuxedo and tails, smiling in front of a baby grand piano.

"He's a musician?"

"Used to be," Lock said from the doorway, startling her. "Before rheumatoid arthritis took that away from me. Can't even play a scale now. It pains me to even try. I keep that piano around to torture myself with what could have been." Lock was smiling, but there was a pained look in his eyes. "Your father and I used to joke about how our bodies betrayed us."

Brooke hadn't known her father had shared the deeply personal struggle with his own disease, a syndrome called FXTAS, with anyone except immediate family. While she struggled to think of something to say, he handed her a hard hat and another to Victor.

"The access point we'll be using is in the basement of the women's dorm. It's empty right now in preparation for the remodel, so we shouldn't have any interruptions."

They followed the dean out into the chilly air, and Victor sent a text as they walked. Brooke was struck again at how lovely the campus was, a series of stately buildings sprinkled over the hills, shrouded in fog that rolled in off the San Francisco Bay. From the highest building, she imagined, a person would have a panoramic view of the entire bay and across the water to the cities of Hayward, Oakland and the infamous hippie town of Berkeley.

"The students have been relocated to our satellite campuses." Lock gestured to the tall building in the distance. "Really there are only a few professors left here, tidying up, and a security detail to keep people out."

"When do the renovations begin?" Victor asked.

"Officially in two weeks." The dean shot a look at the red brick building, rising in a series of peaked gables partially hidden by a cluster of trees. "That's the girls'—" he shook his head "—sorry, women's dormitory. Empty now, and next to it is the library."

She followed him past the graceful columns. The Gage Library. Victor's family really did live in a different stratosphere. Her skin prickled with goose bumps. It was so empty, so silent. The grassy area that should have been sprinkled with students nursing coffees and cramming for tests was deserted and eerily still. She felt a deep longing for the college life that she'd given up after only one semester. After losing her dance career to a knee injury, she'd tried for years to rehab before finally admitting defeat. It seemed like a lifetime before she'd returned to college, but the decision to leave had been easy. There had been no choice with her father being investigated by the police, the press shadowing his every move.

And Tuney.

The man had broken into her hotel room.

He would not stop until her father was disgraced.

She shot a look at Victor, who would also not let go until the truth was revealed.

He must have felt her gaze on him because he turned to look at her, eyes dark in the gloomy morning. He looked completely calm, handsome, self-assured as if he might be a professor strolling the campus on his way to teach a physics class. Hard to fathom that the day before he'd been wire taut, impassioned as he worked to bring the dark-haired lady back to life.

The memory of her lying there, dying, stabbed at Brooke.

She shivered, and Victor took off his jacket and draped it over her, fingers caressing her shoulders as he did. The gesture startled her.

She started to decline but he did not give her the chance, merely strolled forward to ask the dean a question. The jacket smelled of leather and a subtle musky aftershave. In spite of herself she snuggled deeper into the supple material.

Removing a heavy key ring from his pocket, Lock unlocked the front door and they entered an empty room with windows that looked out on the grassy hill and a small patio. Again she fought a feeling of unease. So empty, as if the building was a mother who had lost all of her children to some terrible accident.

Stop it, Brooke. No time for your ridiculous imagination.

"Sad, really," Lock said, his voice loud in the hushed space. "This building has stood largely untouched since the thirties."

The clusters of worn, upholstered chairs were pulled into odd groups and the wooden floor was nicked and scarred by the countless students who had paraded through over the years. A fireplace, blackened inside, crowded one wall.

A few minutes later they were entering a narrow stairwell and descended three flights until they emerged in a cavernous space, dark and smelling of mold. The dean flipped on a light that flickered to life, revealing an empty basement with a set of metal doors at the far end.

He ignored a tiny panel near the door.

"Alarm?" Victor said.

"It's not activated now so the workmen can have free access, but usually the administration takes great pains to ensure no one has access to the tunnel system. You wouldn't believe how much trouble college kids can get into," Lock said.

Victor chuckled. "Yes, I would."

Lock gave him an amused glance. "Your father was amazed that you made it through medical school. He couldn't figure out how someone with a genius IQ could get into so many scrapes."

"My father was kicked out of three colleges before he struck out on his own, so he has little room to talk," Victor said.

Brooke heard the warmth in Victor's voice when he spoke of his father, a sharp contrast to his coolness and efficiency. They had that in common anyway. The doors groaned open, exhaling a waft of cold air.

"Pipes here are disconnected?" Victor said.

"Yes. Otherwise we'd be walking into a sauna right now." Lock put on his hard hat, and Brooke and Victor followed suit.

Brooke tried to give Victor back his jacket, but he refused.

"I've got more body mass to keep me warm," he murmured in her ear, sending tickles up and down her spine as they moved forward.

If it weren't for the meager light provided by a rickety setup of overhead lightbulbs, the darkness would have swallowed them up completely. The tunnel was damp, the walls clammy with moisture. Along either side of the tunnel were long webs of jointed pipes, heavy with rust. The space was so narrow the three of them had to crowd together, and Victor's height left a scant few inches between his head and the light fixtures. Grit scraped under their feet as they shuffled along.

"You see what I mean?" Lock said. "This is the last place anyone would come to hide a painting, especially a valuable one. The conditions in here would destroy a piece immediately."

Brooke felt her heart sink. He was right. Colda would never have risked concealing a Tarkenton in the tunnel. Humidity? Rodents? Water? Any one of them would ruin an oil painting. No one who knew the Tarkenton's value would risk those dangers. It was inconceivable, like throwing the crown jewels into the ocean.

Victor looked around, keeping his head bent to avoid cracking into the pipes around him. He glanced at Brooke as if trying to read her thoughts. She wondered what was going through his mind. If her search ended, he might lose the chance to find out if there was any connection between the missing painting and his wife's death. There wasn't, she was sure, but for some reason having him there was comforting in spite of his distrust of her father.

"Does this tunnel lead to any others?" Victor asked.

The dean pushed on. "You'll have your answer in a few minutes."

They pressed on, and the chill seemed to leach out from the pipes into Brooke's spine. Her hands were cold, skin goose-pimpled. Unless the conditions changed significantly, there was no possibility that the painting was housed in the damp tunnels.

Her hard hat clanked against an elbow of pipe that jutted into the space. The farther they pressed into the chilled darkness, the more on edge she became. "How much farther?" she asked.

Lock stopped. "This is what I wanted you to see." He pointed a gnarled finger ahead and eased back so Victor and Brooke could move closer.

Brooke found herself staring through an old rusted metal grate. She pressed a hand to the iron mesh. Beyond was a ruinous pile of twisted pipes and jagged blocks of concrete. It was completely impassable. The floor was obscured under several inches of murky water.

"Take a look at the padlock," the dean said.

Victor fingered the heavy rusted piece. "Hasn't been opened for a long time."

"Since five years ago when the tunnel collapsed. Wouldn't be any point in going in there anyway."

Brooke suppressed a groan. She'd been so sure that the tunnels held the answers. Proof that the Tarkenton was real, that her father had found a treasure that would obliterate his rocky past and provide a secure future for her brother. In her mind it was a tunnel of light, of hope.

Ahead she saw only ruin.

Victor put a hand on hers, fingers warm against her cold skin. "We should go now."

She nodded, unable to trust her voice.

Dean Lock squeezed past her. "I'm sorry to disappoint you, Ms. Ramsey. It really would be incredible to think there was a buried treasure here, but as you can see it's just not possible."

The pity in his tone was worse than the disappointment stabbing through her. "Thank you anyway," she forced herself to say. Chilled and numb with discouragement, she followed him on the way out.

Victor fell in behind her. "I'm…sorry," he said.

Sorry that her father wouldn't get a second chance? Or sorry that Victor had lost the chance to prove her father was a criminal like he'd always suspected? She did not want to find comfort in his large palm pressed to her back, but nonetheless she did. Must be the impenetrable darkness that made her feel so weak.

She willed her legs to move faster, to get out of that dank place so she could think, but she had no time to do so.

There was an audible snap.

Without warning the lights went out.

FIVE

"What...?" Dean Lock began.

The sudden blackout disoriented Victor. "Stay still," he said. "We don't want anyone falling."

"Must be a power failure," Lock said. "I know the way out. I'll go get a flashlight."

"No," Victor repeated. A fall in these conditions was inevitable. He eased forward and found Brooke, looping his arm around her, ignoring the way she fit nicely against him. She was not trembling, and her voice was steady when she spoke.

"We should wait a minute and see if they come back on," she said.

"Right. Could be a momentary disruption in the power supply." Victor injected an extra dose of firmness into his words, hoping the dean would listen to the advice. In spite of the warning, he heard Lock shuffling forward. Before he could say another word there was a cry of pain and the sound of the man falling.

He groped in the darkness, fighting a surge of

frustration. His doctor skills were worth precisely nothing when he couldn't even see the patient. It reminded him of the spelunking trips Luca strong-armed him into; only, his brother always carried enough gear on their adventures to survive a nuclear winter. And Victor now found himself in a black hole without so much as a matchstick.

He felt around for Lock's leg and was rewarded with a groan.

"I think I twisted my ankle," the dean said, voice hoarse with pain.

"I'm going to go get help. Brooke, can you sit with him?"

She didn't answer.

"Brooke?"

Her voice came from ahead. She'd moved past while he was checking out the dean.

"I'll go," she said. "You need to stay, you're the doctor."

I'm not a doctor anymore, he wanted to snarl, but he kept his voice calm. "Brooke, that's not a good idea."

"I used to play a game like this with my brother. Blindman's bluff. And besides," she said, "I'm shorter than you. Less likely to bang my head."

He would have tried again to make her see reason, but he heard a clang from the basement, a faraway thud of a door swinging open. "Did you hear that?"

She must have, because she stopped moving.

As the lights were abruptly restored, the tunnel flooded back into view.

Victor blinked as his sister strode into view.

"Sorry I'm late, but I just got your text," she said, a sardonic grin on her face. "Wouldn't it be easier to search with the lights on?"

"Funny," Victor said. He looked down at the dean, who had a hand over his eyes. Victor gently probed Lock's ankle while Brooke and Stephanie joined them.

"We were getting a quick tour," Brooke said, "when the lights went out."

"And you were going for help?" Stephanie said.

Brooke's cheeks pinked. "I'm pretty good at bumbling along in the dark."

She was, too, Victor noted. She'd made it nearly to the door by the time Stephanie turned the lights on. It didn't erase his irritation that she'd ignored his advice. With Brooke and Victor's help, Lock got to his feet. "You see?" he said sheepishly. "I told you the tunnels were dangerous."

"I saw an intercom back in the dorm," Stephanie said. "Who can I contact?"

"Press zero and the operator can tell the security people to send a cart for me."

Stephanie left and Victor supported the dean out into the basement, into a service elevator and finally up to the lobby, where he eased into a chair. Brooke perched uneasily on a sofa across from the dean.

Victor paced. His mind was running through what

they'd seen in the tunnels. He felt Brooke's eyes on him. "You should have stayed put. Might have been you that hurt your ankle."

"I've hurt myself plenty of times. I'm a dancer." A shadow crossed her face. "At least, I was."

Half frustrated, half intrigued, he felt the urge to find out every detail of her life.

The arrival of a golf cart interrupted them, and soon the dean was loaded on board. As the two attendants in jumpsuits helped the injured man, Stephanie whispered in Victor's ear.

"You sure?" he said.

Stephanie gave him the irritated look she gave him whenever he questioned her research.

Brooke saw the exchange and raised a questioning eyebrow.

"I apologize for the drama," Lock said with a smile. "Call me if I can help you further."

Victor smiled. "Actually, I think it would be better if we stayed for a few days."

Lock's eyes widened. "What do you mean? What on earth for?"

Brooke was staring at Victor now, blue eyes round with surprise.

"There are a few more things I'd like to look into."

Lock shook his head, wiping at a smudge of rust that marred his shirtsleeve. "You've seen the tunnels. There's no treasure hidden down there."

"Colda had an apartment here on campus," Stephanie said.

Lock started. "How did you know that?"

Stephanie smiled. "We wouldn't be very good treasure hunters if we didn't check out the professor's place." She looked around. "He loved chess, spent a good deal of time in the library, too. All that bears looking into."

Victor noticed the tiny bead of sweat on the dean's temple. Exertion from hobbling out of the tunnels?

"I suppose," Lock said, "but the university security and the police have searched his apartment and, besides, we're not in the business of hosting guests."

Brooke rose from her seat and smiled, a grin that both mesmerized Victor and made something tingle through his veins.

"Of course you are," she said, with a sweeping gesture. "You've got an entire building here for your women guests. And there are plenty of vacancies at the moment."

"Another for the men, right across the way," Victor added.

"No," Lock said. "The administration will never allow it."

Victor cast a glance toward the stately columns of the library. He didn't want to play the card, but Lock gave him no choice. "I heard Bayside was interested in purchasing the land behind the university for a new science building." A worthy endeavor. Very worthy. Very expensive. Gage family money would be crucial in such an effort. It was essentially blackmail, but he knew Lock needed some motivation to grant his request.

Dean Lock heard the unspoken message. He lowered his head for a moment, rubbed his face with his good hand before he met Victor's eyes again. "You've got to be out by demolition day. You can't stay here tonight. I've got to inform the university president. Come to my office tomorrow morning and I'll give you the keys to Colda's place and the dormitories."

"Thank you for your cooperation," Victor said.

Lock shook his head. "Isn't that like the barracuda thanking the squid?"

They watched the dean bump away, seated in the back of the cart.

"I'm going to pack up some gear and update Luca about our college overnighter," Stephanie said with a mischievous grin. "He's not going to believe this, and it's going to make him insane not being here."

Victor and Brooke followed. "I'll drive you back to the hotel. We'll return in the morning."

Brooke caught his arm and turned him to face her. "I don't understand. The dean is right. There couldn't be a Tarkenton in that tunnel. Do you really think we'll find it in Colda's office?"

"No. I imagine the police have thoroughly searched that, and whoever else is after the painting."

"Then why are we staying?"

He noticed a cobweb trapped in the coppery strands of her bangs. He gently removed it, feeling the soft silk of her hair. For a moment, he forgot the question until she repeated it.

"We're staying because the power didn't fail when we were in that tunnel," he said.

Brooke frowned. "What do you mean?"

"Stephanie told me the switch was off. Someone did it on purpose."

"Who would do that?"

"We can rule out the dean, for one, and there are no students around, no staff."

Her face clouded. "Then someone else doesn't want us here."

"And I can only think of one reason why. There really is a treasure here that somebody wants for themselves."

They walked to his car in silence, the fog enveloping them in moisture. It wasn't until he checked her room for unwanted visitors and prepared to leave that she asked the question.

"What is your nickname? The one your father gave you?"

Victor sighed. "Sea Tiger. It's a catchy name for the barracuda."

She cocked her head. "Why? Your teeth aren't sharp and pointy."

He laughed. "It's not an altogether flattering comparison. Barracudas are relentless when they want something. They don't sleep, and you can't distract them when they're fixed on their prey."

"So you're relentless?"

His gaze wandered over her face, lingering on her lips. "Only when I need something." He walked away, wondering why he felt a strange need coursing through his heart at that very moment, a need that had nothing to do with a missing painting.

Brooke hardly slept. She awoke the next morning with gritty eyes and tangled sheets. A shower did little to revive her as she tried to organize her thoughts. They were going to camp out at the university and do what? Search Leo Colda's room? It seemed to her unlikely that they would find anything the police or the university personnel who had gone to look for their missing professor hadn't.

And Victor had led the charge, pressuring the dean to allow it.

She recalled the intensity that smoldered in his eyes.

Sea Tiger.

Relentless.

And if he found evidence that somehow linked her father to wrongdoing?

She knew her father was a man of principle, an innocent in the robbery, yet he had been secretive of late.

Scribbling notes, closeted in his study, leaving her and Denise to wonder.

No, she told herself, twisting off the shower faucet. *Dad isn't guilty of anything, and I'm going to get his painting back to prove it.*

She had to. Her father was failing, and his reputation was the only thing he had left. Finding a Tarkenton would be a coup that no one could take away from him. The sale of it would help her bring Tad back home and maybe pay for someone to help with the challenges of his Fragile X Syndrome. She could not afford to fail. Tad was counting on her, too.

Chin up, Brooke.

With her few belongings stowed in a small bag, Brooke headed down to find Victor already waiting in the lobby. He leaned against the wall, in black jeans and a tucked-in T-shirt. Black jacket, loose-fitting. He could have been a tourist, or a man waiting for his date, but for the intensity on his face. Her pulse edged up a notch as she joined him.

"Morning," he said. "Did you get any sleep?"

"No. You?"

He shook his head as they walked to the car. "I don't need much."

"Is that the barracuda in you?"

He shot a look at her and then smiled, an expression that lifted the dark shadows from his face. "I have a hard time shutting off my mind."

She picked up the file tucked neatly between the seats in Victor's Mercedes. "Last night's project?"

"Research," he said. "Go ahead and look."

She riffled through the papers, which included a brief biography of L. Tarkenton and some glossy photos of several of his oil paintings.

"I need you to tell me about the missing painting,"

he said. "There are no references to the one you described that I could find."

"I'm not surprised. Dad's spent most of his life sniffing out hints about it. It's called *The Contemplative Lady.* The subject is a young woman looking out the window of a drawing room. It's done in oils. My father found reference to it in one of Tarkenton's letters but no one has ever found proof that Tarkenton actually went beyond the planning stages of the work, until my father came home with the painting from that estate sale. It's unsigned, but he's sure it's the Lady."

"Are you sure?"

She hesitated only a moment. "Yes. I'm not a trained art historian, but I've spent four years immersed in my father's world."

"What happened to dancing?"

The car suddenly felt very small. "I got a scholarship to a dance academy in New York but I injured my knee."

"So you came home?"

She flushed. "Yes. I worked some part-time jobs and spent years trying to find a passion again. Finally, I started college, which was a terrible mistake."

"Why?"

"My brother had trouble. He can't control his anger sometimes. He was sent to a group home. If I had stayed home, he might not have gotten so bad." She shook her head, wondering why she'd told him any of the whole messy story. Desperate to change the train of conversation she noticed another file, stuck in the pocket of the driver's side door. "What's in that one?"

Victor stared at the road ahead, accelerating through a yellow light. "More research."

"May I take a look?"

"Nothing you'd want to see."

Her pulse quickened. "I guess I'd better take a look anyway."

He shot her a look but she could not read the expression behind the serious demeanor. Slowly he removed it and handed it to her.

Her heart sank as she scanned the pages. "What is this?"

"It's a copy of Tuney's report to me after he finished his investigation into the museum theft. Cops determined the mastermind was familiar with the delivery schedule even though that was only provided to the curators and security people a few days before. When the truck pulled into the lot, the thief was waiting."

She forced out the words. "But there was no proof of my father's involvement. Lock could have been behind it."

"There was not enough proof to pin it on either one. I was just refreshing myself on the details. Take a look at the second set of papers."

With fingers gone suddenly cold she found the pages. "Phone records? From my house?"

"Not official. That would be illegal."

She forced a calm tone even though her insides were churning. How much had he pried into the private life of her family? "Then how did you get them?"

He sighed. "My sister is very…effective at collecting information. She called in a favor. Cop told her, off the record, that Colda called your house in San Diego once the week before he disappeared."

The breath seemed to bottle up in her lungs. "It doesn't mean anything. They were colleagues, Colda was evaluating a painting for him. It makes sense that he would call our house."

"Then why was the phone call only five seconds in duration?"

"What?"

"Cop said Colda hung up the phone immediately after it was answered."

"Hung up?" Her head spun. "Was he worried that someone was eavesdropping?"

"Not sure, but he was worried about something. Seems he booked a flight out of SFO."

Nerves tingled along her spine. "What was the destination?"

"San Diego."

She swallowed hard. "He was coming to see my father?"

He nodded grimly. "But he never made it on that plane."

SIX

He saw her clutch at the little gold cross around her neck, smoothing it in her fingers.

"Do you…" She cleared her throat. "Do you think Professor Colda is dead?"

He wanted to tell her that in his mind there was no doubt about it, but oddly he could not bring himself to say it. "We'll have to see. No sign of foul play. The cops floated the idea that he left for the break. His classes don't start up for another two weeks at the satellite location, so they think he could have gone on a vacation."

"But you don't think so?"

Victor tried for a gentle tone. "It's strange that he would have paid for a plane ticket and not shown."

Her eyes closed and he saw her mouth move, and he wondered if she was praying. *Your God won't hear you,* he thought. He hadn't heard Jennifer, and there was no one more deserving of answered prayer than her.

Brooke sighed, a soft, gentle sound that took him

instantly back to the memory of where he'd first seen her. Several months before the crash, Jennifer was meeting with then-curator Lock at the museum to arrange to take her middle schoolers on a trip. Victor went along, left to wander through paintings he had no interest in, when he came upon Brooke. He hadn't known her name. Her hair was different, face fuller then.

She stared with rapt attention at a small Degas, a painting of a ballerina, ethereal and graceful. It was not the painting that captured Victor's attention, but the look on Brooke's face—sadness, longing, painful disappointment laid bare in that moment. She'd probably been dealing with the loss of her dancing career. Home for a quick visit to her father perhaps. He'd stood frozen, captivated by the sheer nakedness of the emotion, uncertain what, if anything, he should do about it, until another visitor came close and Brooke scurried away.

In the years after Jennifer's death he'd thought about that face, pondered how she had shown on her face the worst emotions that crowded into his heart after the accident. It was all written there, naked, for anyone to see, except one emotion was missing. Rage.

Her father may very well be a thief, Victor reminded himself, rekindling the anger in his own heart. It didn't matter what Brooke felt or did. He needed to find the truth.

But what if the truth about Donald changed Brooke

Ramsey? Would it pain Victor to see her face hardened by the same anger that turned his own heart to stone? He tried to shake off the idiotic thoughts.

A movement in the rearview mirror caught his eye. He stiffened at the sight of the motorcycle a few car lengths behind, the driver's face hidden behind the tinted faceplate of the helmet. "I saw the same guy on the motorcycle when I drove over to get you this morning."

Brooke peeked into the side mirror instead of turning around. *Good girl,* he thought.

"So now there's someone following us?"

"Maybe. Let's find out." Abruptly he changed lanes, eliciting a honk from the car behind him. He pushed his way over to the right-hand lane and turned down a narrow, one-way street. Victor's heart was beating fast, eyes intent on the rearview mirror as he slowed the car.

He could be mistaken.

It could be a different motorcycle than the one he'd seen.

Or paranoia born of the shooting at his office.

It took a few moments before the motorcycle made the turn, also.

Victor's blood pumped faster, as he strained in the rearview mirror to get a glimpse of the man's face.

"Is it Tuney?" Brooke's eyes were riveted to the side-view mirror.

"That was my first thought, but the driver's too tall to be Tuney."

"What now?" she said.

Victor's stomach tightened in determination. "Now we find out how good the guy is. Buckle up."

Brooke clutched the door with one hand and her seat belt with the other.

He waited until the motorcycle closed the gap to one car length, then he increased his speed, turning one left and then another until they were back on the main drag. San Francisco's middle-of-the-day traffic was not terrible because most people who lived in the city didn't bother to drive, as parking spaces were expensive and hard to come by.

He slowed just enough to let the motorcyclist ease closer.

Come on, buddy. You've almost got me, don't you?

Victor began an intricate series of lane changes and moved in and out of side streets, doubling back and moving forward until Brooke gasped.

"I'm getting dizzy."

He pulled into a one-way street, hemmed in by tall, old warehouses on either side. The car idled while they waited to see if Victor's tricks had worked.

The motorcycle turned in behind them once more.

"Guy's determined and not a bad driver. He must be somewhat familiar with the city. There's a place just ahead, an old box factory. We'll lose him there unless he knows this city better than I do."

"What if he does know it better than you do?"

Victor shrugged. "Then we'll have the chance to

get to know each other pretty soon. Be ready to get a plate number if you can."

Brooke clutched her seat belt with one hand. "How do you know this area so well?"

"We lived in San Francisco for decades. My brother never met an abandoned building he didn't want to photograph." He had to fight to keep himself from hitting the gas too hard.

Keep it cool.

Another block and he accelerated and flipped a quick left turn, moving quickly enough to ease into a narrow alley before the motorcycle. He pushed the car faster and jerked it into a space behind a crumbling brick facade, intended to artfully conceal trash dumpsters.

Victor held his breath, pulse pounding, and he could tell by Brooke's rigid posture that she was doing the same.

One second.

Three.

Thirty seconds later and they heard it, the rumble of a motorcycle engine.

It grew louder and then roared past.

Brooke exhaled. "Sorry I didn't get a plate number," she said, voice high and tense.

"It's all right. At least we lost him for the moment."

She uncurled her fingers from the seat belt. "That was some driving."

He felt unaccountably pleased at her comment until she added, "For a barracuda."

* * *

The dean greeted Victor, Brooke and Stephanie with a weary smile when they arrived, and gestured to his ankle, encased in an elastic bandage. "Bad sprain," he said. "I know what you're thinking. I should have stayed put when the lights went out down there."

Victor shrugged and smiled politely, but Brooke could tell that was exactly what he was thinking. She also had the feeling that Victor did not completely trust Dean Lock.

He took the keys to Colda's place the dean offered and thanked him again.

Brooke added her thanks, also. She felt the tingle of excitement. Maybe Colda had left some sort of indication of where he'd stowed the painting. It was a long shot, extremely long. She wished she could search by herself, comb every square inch of the campus and restore her father's good name without relying on Victor and Stephanie to help, but without them she wouldn't have gotten anywhere.

God would help her see it through, in spite of Victor's doubts. She felt certain about that.

Lock looked away for a moment, apparently studying the oil painting of a desert mesa on his wall. "Colda was living in the Professor House. That's the hall where the staff who choose to reside on campus are housed. The House is undergoing only minor upgrades, since it's a fairly new structure, but the resident professors have all been relocated for the time being." He paused. "I'm going to send someone to accompany you."

Brooke wasn't surprised. The staff wouldn't be happy to hear about strangers given carte blanche to enter their building. They heard a knock.

"Morning," Tuney said, shuffling into the room. "Lovely day for a treasure hunt, isn't it?"

Brooke gasped, her stomach instantly in knots. "What are you doing here?"

Tuney offered a smile. "Dean Lock invited me to be your escort."

They all turned to look at the dean. "Mr. Tuney was hired by the University Board to locate Leo Colda."

Victor's eyes swiveled between Tuney and Lock and back to Tuney. "So you're employed by Bayside? Why didn't you tell us that before?"

Tuney shrugged. "I'm not in the business of handing out information, just acquiring it. I've already been through Colda's office with a fine-tooth comb, talked to his students, including the one who saw him exiting the tunnels. You're going to find zippo in his place, trust me."

"Then why are you coming along?" Stephanie said, eyes flashing. Brooke heard the challenge in her voice and no trace of fear. Brooke wondered what it would feel like to be fearless. *Must run in the Gage family,* she thought as she watched brother and sister staring at Tuney with similar expressions of irritation.

Tuney fired back a sardonic smile.

"You know about the shooting at my office?" Victor said to Lock. "How Tuney hired someone to follow Brooke?"

"I understand Colda tried to make contact with the Ramsey family before he disappeared. It seems a natural step for someone investigating to follow the trail." His glance flicked to Brooke and then back to Victor. "The university has heard from the police that there are no leads on the shooting of Tuney's cohort."

Brooke thought she heard the slightest note of disdain in Lock's choice of the word *cohort*. Could it be that Tuney had been forced on Lock by the administration?

Lock cleared his throat. "My orders are to have Tuney accompany you in your investigations, so that's what I'm going to do. He won't get in your way, I'm sure."

The smug look on Tuney's face made Brooke quiver inside, but she knew there was no point in resisting.

"I trust you have no problem with Tuney's assistance in this matter?" Lock said, directing his gaze at Brooke. "You have nothing to hide, do you?"

Do you?

She thought about her father's secretive behavior. It grated on her that she hadn't known he'd sent the painting to Colda. Why hadn't he trusted her with the information? She swallowed the doubts and lifted her chin. "Of course not. The more eyes the better."

"Great," Tuney said, fishing a key from his pocket. "Then let's go over to Colda's place. It's a dump, but it should be interesting to see if you can find something I didn't."

With a sinking feeling in her stomach, Brooke headed out into the chilly morning, following Stephanie and Victor.

Tuney lingered behind to exchange words with the dean.

Victor's jaw was tight, strides quick and angry. Stephanie and Brooke had to jog to keep up. "I don't like having someone looking over my shoulder, especially someone I don't trust. I never should have..." He broke off.

What? Brooke wondered. Hired a man like Tuney all those years before? Did he feel like Brooke did, that putting Tuney on a case was like dripping blood into shark-infested waters? She wanted to be angry at him for hiring such a man, but she wasn't sure she would have behaved differently if it was her loved one who died at the hands of someone who got away scot-free.

Her thoughts surprised her. Understanding for this man? A man who would be elated to pin a death on her innocent father? She quickened her pace, trying to leave the thoughts behind. They arrived on the front porch of a tidy two-story bungalow, brick sides edged in ivy. It was neat and well tended, charmingly old in appearance but newly renovated, as evidenced by the double-paned windows and smart trim.

Tuney finally joined them and unlocked the door, standing aside with a flourish. "Colda's is upstairs, the suite at the end of the hallway." They climbed the stairs, trailed down a darkened corridor, and he unlocked the interior door and stepped back, allowing the others to enter first.

Brooke gasped.

"Has it been tossed?" Stephanie said.

Tuney laughed. "No, the guy's just a slob of epic proportions."

Slob was an understatement. Stacks of magazines and books dotted the wood floors. A tangle of ivy cascaded from a pot down the stuffed bookcase, both plant and books coated with a layer of dust. Piles of books filled every available corner, and the windows were plastered with sticky notes and tattered bits of paper taped here and there.

"Hard to believe Colda is a professor, isn't it?" Tuney said, fingering a stack of comic books. "Lived more like a vagrant. Students said he was flighty. He had no sense of time. One time he was in the library and forgot what time it was. One of his teaching assistants had to go find him so he could teach class."

Tuney went on, but Brooke wasn't listening. Her gaze was drawn to the wall next to a battered dining table, covered with stacks of newspapers.

"That's it," she said.

Victor and Stephanie continued to prowl around the space and paid her no attention so she said it louder.

"There." Something in her tone made them both stop.

She pointed to the small, framed picture above the dining-room table. "That's *The Contemplative Lady,*" she said with a sigh. "Well, a reproduction anyway." Even though it wasn't the real thing, the genius of the work came through. The look on the lady's face as she gazed wistfully out the window, the chessboard forgotten to the lure of the sunlight playing over the garden. Was she pining for her love? Chafing against the constraints of being a woman of the 1800s? Wishing for a life somewhere outside those walls?

Victor broke her reverie, taking out his iPhone to snap a picture. "Well, at least we've got a nice visual on what we're looking for. Why would he hang a reproduction?"

Brooke took a picture with her phone, as well.

Stephanie scanned the walls. "It's the only artwork he's got in the place."

"I wondered that, too," Tuney said. "I'll admit, I was taken in at first. I'm no art guy, so it took me a minute to realize it was a fake."

"He must have painted it himself." Brooke broke into a smile. "At least it proves my father really did contact Colda about the painting, otherwise he wouldn't have known what it looked like."

Tuney shook his head. "Doesn't prove the painting

was ever really here. We still don't have a Tarkenton or any clue about what happened to Colda."

Brooke sighed. He was right, but in her mind it was another step in the right direction.

Victor turned his attention back to the overflowing file cabinet. "Looks like Colda kept every scrap of paper he ever ran across."

"Mostly bills, some past due, a few articles about obscure art-related stuff." Tuney cleared some newspapers off the small sofa and settled in, his feet up on the coffee table. "I'm just going to take a little nap, don't mind me. Wake me if you find something."

Stephanie shot him a look.

Brooke tore herself away from the painting and headed for the bedroom, where she and Victor lifted up the mattress and throw rugs, searched the closet and drawers with no success. Brooke found her eyes wandering back to the Tarkenton reproduction just visible through the doorway. Something about it poked at her.

"Got an idea?" Victor asked.

She started, realizing she'd been standing motionless, staring. "No, nothing. Just something about it that I can't figure out."

He came closer, face intent. "Might be your instincts trying to tell you something. In my experience, it's a good idea to listen."

Her nerves began to tingle but she could not decide if it was something about the painting, or the proximity to this enigmatic man. Stephanie called to them from the kitchen and they joined her there.

She waved a hand at the sink piled with crusted dishes. "Colda could have used a housekeeper."

"Or a sanitation company," Victor said with disgust.

"Look at the whiteboard," Stephanie said.

They squinted at a series of letters and numbers. "5, 7, 2."

"Telephone number?" Brooke suggested.

"Room numbers," Tuney called from the living room. "Colda couldn't remember where he was supposed to be for each class. He wrote it down to help himself but that didn't work. The admin finally moved all his classes to the same room so he wouldn't keep missing them."

Brooke sighed and patted Stephanie's arm. "It was a good idea anyway."

Stephanie shook her head. "Not good enough."

The three exchanged glances and Brooke understood.

Be careful what you say.

Tuney is monitoring every word.

Brooke returned to the living room, feeling more discouraged with each passing minute. Her gaze returned again to the lady in the painting.

If only you could talk, she thought.

If only.

SEVEN

Victor's back was aching and his stomach growling by late afternoon. They'd stopped just long enough to eat the sandwiches Stephanie had gone to get. Going through files, boxes and bags looking for some indication of where Colda had stashed the painting or where he had disappeared to had yielded nothing but clouds of dust. Victor did not mind the searching—he'd spent hundreds of hours as a med student and surgeon winnowing out the tiniest references to surgical procedures that might inform his own treatment of his patients. He had to admit that he didn't like floundering around in the vague hope of finding a treasure with only the flimsiest of clues to guide them. And above all, he didn't like having someone watching.

But hadn't he paid the man four years before to do exactly that? And truth be told, he hadn't cared about the methodology. But now, when it was Tuney determined to bring down Brooke's father, he felt uncomfortable.

Maybe because Ramsey's red-haired daughter intrigued him? Made him begin to question his own need for vengeance?

Victor chalked up his uncharacteristic emotionalism to fatigue. A whole day wasted.

They continued to plow through the mess for another few hours until some silent understanding passed between them and they convened in the front room. Discouragement was written on Brooke's face. Stephanie wore her usual expression of calm, but Victor knew she was as frustrated as he was.

Tuney lifted an eyebrow. "Leaving so soon? It took me three days to get through the mess."

Victor held back his rising temper. "What did you learn from the witness? The one who saw Colda leaving the tunnel?"

"Nothing much. She said she was down in the basement, moving a box of sorority stuff and she saw Colda coming out of the same area you went into yesterday."

"The tunnel goes nowhere. It's impassable."

"I know. That's why I don't credit the story that he's hidden anything down there. The police took a dog down to sniff around, more to appease the administration than anything else. They found nothing but a dead rat carcass."

"What's your theory, then?" Stephanie asked, finger-combing some bits of plaster out of her short, tousled hair.

"If there really is such a painting, I think Colda made off with it, tried to skip town and Donald killed him." He stared at Brooke. "I think the painting is stashed somewhere off campus, or maybe your father already has it back."

Brooke shook her head. "Then why would I be here looking for it?"

"Because your father didn't clue you in, did he?"

She looked away. "There wasn't anything to tell me. He doesn't have the painting."

"But you can't explain the phone call to your house from Colda, the ticket he bought to San Diego but never got on the flight?"

"I don't have to explain it," she said, hands on hips. "I've never met Colda, but judging from his place here, he's eccentric, to say the least."

Tuney seemed to weigh something in his mind. "Your father took a trip a few weeks back. Stopped right across the bay."

She started. "Yes. He went to the library to study some archived letters."

"Where?"

"U.C. Berkeley."

"True, but he made one other stop. Here at Bayside, to visit his old pal. Only, Colda wasn't around, so they left without meeting."

"Okay, sounds innocent enough," Victor put in. "Donald wanted an update on the appraisal of his painting. Natural that he'd look Colda up while he was in town."

Tuney shrugged. "Sounds normal on the surface, but I talked to the cafeteria manager. She knew

Colda well because he'd order the same thing every day, grilled cheese and tomato sandwich with black coffee. She says Colda was indeed on campus the day and time Donald came to visit. She remembers because Colda asked for his meal to go, something he'd never done in the ten years she'd known him."

Brooke crossed her arms. "I don't see what you're getting at."

"He's trying to figure out why, if Colda was on campus, he didn't want to meet with your father," Victor said.

Brooke gaped. "I have no idea."

"It's suspicious," Victor said. "You've got to admit that."

"I don't have to admit anything. My father is a good man and you can spin all the conspiracy theories you want." Brooke walked to the door. "I need some fresh air."

Victor sighed. "I wasn't spinning theories," he said to no one. "We've got to look at all the facts."

"I don't think Brooke sees it that way," Stephanie said. "And frankly, if it was our dad, I think I'd be feeling the same. I'll see you outside."

Victor felt Tuney's eyes on him. "She's not going to see things clearly where her father is concerned. We're going to have to ferret out the truth whether she likes it or not," Tuney said.

We? Victor saw Brooke out the window, sitting in a meager beam of late-afternoon sunlight, slight shoulders hunched as if from bearing a heavy weight.

If her father was unmasked, then the person who planned the robbery would finally be punished.

And Brooke Ramsey would be destroyed.

Brooke wanted to be alone, to hide herself away from everyone and think, but there was no time as she and Stephanie made their way into the empty women's dormitory. She sensed that Stephanie wanted to say something, but Brooke avoided eye contact. One kind word from the woman, and she knew she would dissolve into tears.

At the heart of her anguish was the knowledge that Tuney was right. Her father hadn't "clued her in." She hadn't known that he'd visited Bayside. He hadn't mentioned it and neither had Denise. The omission burned inside her. As soon as she could get a moment alone, she intended to call them and find out why.

They located a suitable empty room, a long rectangular space with nothing more than three twin beds, a tiny sink area, a battered desk with an equally battered chair and a bulletin board still sporting a picture of a handsome man who Brooke assumed was a movie actor. A dried flower was pinned to the wall. The remnant of a boyfriend's offering? The space was painted in a shade of yellow that had probably once been cheerful.

Stephanie set her duffel bag on one of the beds.

"Cozy," she said, plopping down her sleeping bag and an extra she'd brought for Brooke. "Bathroom is down the hall. Let's go find that brother of mine and get some food. I'm starving."

Brooke sank down on the bed and pulled out her cell phone. "You go. I wanted to call home and check in."

Stephanie hesitated. "You sure?"

"Yes."

Stephanie studied her for a moment, dark eyes intense like Victor's, before she nodded and left.

When she was alone, Brooke dialed. It rang and rang with no answer. She prowled the room with restless steps, stopping to look out the window into the darkening sky like the contemplative lady in Tarkenton's painting. She pulled up the picture on her cell phone again, staring at the small image. Something preyed on her mind, nibbling at the corners. Something wrong. Something out of place.

Her thoughts would not cooperate, and the quiet of the deserted dormitory enveloped her with smothering silence. A walk might clear her thoughts. She'd be safe if she ventured no farther than the courtyard. Before the walls closed in around her she found her way outside, cool air bathing her face. In the distance, the hills were still visible against a clouded sky. It was such a melancholy sight she wished she could put it to dance right at that very moment, to let her inner turmoil find expression in the glorious high release or a twisting spiral.

A low brick wall encircled the place and her heart

skipped to see a man sitting there, facing away from her in the pool of light from a single lamppost.

Tuney.

She turned to go when he saw her.

"Settled in?"

She nodded, intending to leave without further comment, when she detected something different in his face, a soft expression she didn't understand. A trick of the moonlight? He was holding a newspaper, open to the sports section.

He noticed her eyeing it. "Reading about spring training. Fran was a real baseball nut."

Brooke was startled. The gentle look. The wistful expression. "She was a good friend?"

He folded the newspaper with a snap. "Fran was an all-right gal. Never complained, and she had plenty in her life to gripe about. Always said she was happy to be standing on her own two feet even wearing cheap shoes." He laughed.

"I'm sorry about her death," Brooke said.

"Me, too. It's always grated on me that good people get the short end of the stick. Plenty of scumbags and users out there in the world, but Fran wasn't like that. So why does she have to take a bullet?" He shook his head. "No justice in the world."

"I didn't know, it didn't seem from the way you talked about her that you two were close."

Tuney got to his feet. "What difference does that make? She didn't deserve to take a bullet just because she was following you around."

"No, she didn't."

He kicked at a broken chunk of brick. "Anyone that could put up with an old coot like me was some kind of special."

"Did she have family?"

He shook his head. "Said she was better off without anyone." He made a great show of folding the newspaper into a small bundle and tucking it under his arm before he fired a look at her. "Maybe she was right. Family can get you into all kinds of trouble."

She knew he was talking about her father. "I don't want to argue." She turned to go. "I'm sorry about your loss."

He stopped her. "I'm not saying it's your fault. My old man wasn't what I thought he was either. Didn't see that until he walked out of my life when I was nine. "

Brooke felt as though she'd been slapped. "You'll find it interesting that it was my mother that left us, Mr. Tuney. My father has been both parents to me."

Tuney considered for a moment. "Doesn't matter. My dad used me and my mom, just like your old man is using you."

Blood rushed to her cheeks. "I've got to go."

"You're just a pawn, honey, and the sooner you realize that the better."

"Good night, Mr. Tuney."

"'Night."

She felt his gaze following her as she entered the dorm again. She did not want to think of her mother, who was the real betrayer of their family. Shadows hugged the walls, and she hastened her pace. Her room was gloomy, so she snapped on the small lamps and sank down on the bed, dialing her home phone once more.

Still no answer.

As she lay down on the bed, Tuney's words circled in her mind.

Just a pawn.

It wasn't true. Her father would never use her. He was a stubborn man, wrapped up in a love of art that sometimes felt stronger than his love for her. Maybe her mother felt the same, and the feeling caused her to leave.

No. Mom left because she couldn't handle Tad, a kid the rest of the world labeled "mentally deficient."

Her fingers tapped in the number before she had time to think it out. The director of the group home answered and put her through to her brother.

"Hi, Taddy. How are you today?"

"Hi, Brooke."

Tad told her about the new pad and pen set Aunt Denise brought him and the upcoming outing to a community play. She listened to him babble on, her heart swelling up inside her.

"It's gonna be bedtime soon. You sing it?" he asked.

Her throat thickened. "Okay." She began to sing softly, the "Take Me Out to the Ball Game" song that had remained Tad's favorite since he was five years old. Now at twenty-two, he still asked for it.

"Will you take me home soon?" Tad asked.

The question that had haunted her since Tad's anger issues boiled over, leaving her father unable to handle him. Things had come to a head when she'd gone off to college to start a new life. Maybe if Brooke had been home instead of trying to improve her own life, she could have helped, and maybe, just maybe, Tad wouldn't have lashed out. He didn't mean to, he never meant to, but he was a child trapped in an adult body.

"Will you?" Tad repeated.

"Yes, honey. Soon as I can. When I come back from San Francisco, we'll go see a baseball game." She whispered good-night and clicked off the phone, gasping when she saw Victor standing in the doorway holding a paper bag. His face was uncertain.

"Excuse me." He held up the bag. "Didn't think you should stay alone, so we brought dinner in." He shifted slightly. "Nice singing."

She shrugged, face flaming. "My brother, Tad. He likes the song."

"How old?"

"Twenty-two." She saw his eyebrows rise in surprise. "He has Fragile X Syndrome."

Victor nodded. "Mentally disabled."

Brooke clenched her jaw, hating the words. "He's okay. They take good care of him at the facility. I'm going to bring him home when we can afford to hire a caregiver to watch him while I work. I teach dance classes, so it doesn't pay too well."

"Your aunt Denise can't care for Tad?"

"She's got her hands full with my father. He has FXTAS. It's a genetic disorder." She was surprised as the words tumbled out.

"I've read about it. Tremor Ataxia Syndrome, related to Fragile X but the patients can have no problem, extremely high IQs even, until their fifties when…" He broke off.

"When they develop tremors, balance problems and dementia." She looked away.

"Tough thing to live with." Victor put the bag down on the table and parceled out sandwiches and chips, arranging the napkins and rearranging them. "I didn't know what you liked so I went for turkey and Swiss."

"That's fine. Thank you."

She went to the window and toyed with the curtain, wondering why she'd spilled the family's dark genetic secrets to Victor Gage. Was he examining her now? Looking for signs of the FXTAS in her? She stilled her hands. "I talked with Tuney. I think he was in love with Fran."

"Didn't let on about that back in your hotel room."

"No. I don't think he's the kind of man that would," she said thoughtfully. "He said I'm being kept in the dark by my father, that I'm just a pawn in this whole game between him and Colda."

Victor shoved his hands in his pockets. "And what do you think?"

She stared through blurry eyes. "I don't know anymore," she said, feeling the tears threaten. "I only want to find the painting and go home because I love my father and I'm trying to hold what's left of my family together. That's my whole motivation. Can you understand that?"

After a hesitation he nodded. "Yes, I can."

Swallowing hard, she joined him at the table as Stephanie entered.

"Hi, roomie," she said, slicking back her damp hair. "I tried out the showers, and you'll be happy to know there's plenty of hot water."

In spite of her worry, Brooke smiled and they started in on their sandwiches. After a few pleasantries, the conversation faltered until they were eating in silence. Brooke's mind went back to Tuney.

You're just a pawn.

Why hadn't her father or Denise told her about their visit to Colda?

A pawn.

The word circled in her head.

Pawn.

She stood so suddenly the bag of chips fell to the floor, scattering the contents across the worn tile.

Victor sat, sandwich frozen on the way to his mouth, staring at her.

"What it is?" Stephanie said.

"I just figured out what's wrong with the painting, the one in Colda's apartment."

EIGHT

Victor couldn't understand Brooke's chatter as she thumbed her phone to life, but the excitement on her face was undeniable. It lit something inside him and his breath grew short.

"It's the board, the chessboard in the painting," she said, coming between them and laying her phone on the table so they could both see. Squeezed in, her soft shoulder against his and the sweet smell of her hair made his stomach quiver. He shifted slightly and refocused on the tiny screen.

"I knew there was something different about it, but I didn't put it together until just this minute. Colda's painting of the chessboard is different in these four squares." She used a pencil to point to the screen. "*The Contemplative Lady* shows a chessboard with pieces in the initial positions—the rook, knight, bishop, queen, king, bishop, knight and rook all in the first row. The second row…"

Stephanie interrupted. "Is for the pawns, yes, but there are four black pawns on the wrong side of the board. I didn't notice before."

"Colda put black ones on the white side." Victor's eyes widened. "He painted them wrong on purpose?"

"I can't see him making that mistake unless he did it intentionally," Brooke said. "There are definitely four black pawns where they don't belong."

"Are you sure? Can you remember the original that well?" he said.

Brooke laughed, a silvery sound. "I spent hours examining that painting, but if you don't believe me," she said, pulling a photocopy from her backpack. "Here's a photo of the painting my father bought at the estate sale."

Victor looked, then leaned back with a whistle. "Sure enough, but what does it mean? Could be Colda's little joke? The guy is odd, to say the least."

No one answered. Instead they stared fixedly at the screen.

"Four pawns out of place," he said thoughtfully. "If we look at rows, that's one in the first row, one in the second, one in the third and one in the fourth. Does that scream a message to anyone?"

Stephanie paced the room. "I can't think of one."

"How about the columns? I don't remember much about chess but the columns are lettered, right? *A* through *H*?"

"Okay, let's factor that in," he said. "The first row has an out-of-place pawn in the *G* column. Row two has one in the *A* position. Third row has another pawn in the *G* column and row four has a misplaced piece in column *E*." He pulled a piece of paper from his briefcase and started jotting.

Victor felt a shock ripple through him as if he'd been touched by an exposed wire. "It's the column letters. Rearrange them using the row numbers. Column *A,* row two, so we put *A* in the second spot. Column *E,* four, so the letter *E* goes in the fourth position, and column *G* has pawns in the first and third positions, so the *G*s go there."

The two women stared at the paper as he wrote it out.

G-A-G-E.

For once, Stephanie looked completely astonished and Brooke's face shone with excitement. "Maybe he was leaving a message about where he hid the painting."

"In Gage Library?" Victor said, going to the window and peering out into the darkness. "How would he do that without anyone noticing?"

Brooke shook her head. "I'm not sure, but there's a reason he spelled this out."

"For whom?" Stephanie said. "And why?"

"Maybe for himself," Brooke suggested. "He forgot things all the time, maybe this was a refresher in case he couldn't remember where he'd hidden it or how to get there."

Stephanie gaped. "This is like an Indiana Jones movie."

Victor's and Brooke's eyes locked and they both laughed.

"What?" Stephanie demanded. "You don't think this is really some code, do you? A clue in some crazy treasure hunt? It could be unrelated, just some inside joke Colda used to amuse himself."

"Yes," he agreed.

"And the library is nowhere near the spot where Colda was seen exiting the tunnels."

"Also true," Victor said.

"So we're just going to ignore that fact?" she pressed.

"No," Victor said, pulling out his laptop. "We're going to research the old campus until we find out the connection. If there is any."

Stephanie sighed and sat down at the table, turning on her own laptop. "This isn't going to be easy. The records are old. Much of the campus was destroyed in a fire along with the records two decades ago."

"Good thing you're persistent," he said with a chuckle.

"Like trying to find the proverbial needle in the haystack," she said.

"Or a treasure in a tunnel," Brooke said.

Victor's spirits rose. It was a new avenue to investigate. Whether or not it led to another dead end remained to be seen. He found himself surprised that he enjoyed the camaraderie. He could ordinarily go days without seeing or talking to anyone except for his brother and sister. Normally he was content to be alone. Not this time.

They hooked up a printer, and when their efforts

yielded anything of interest, they produced a hard copy, which Brooke perused, papers fanned out across the bed.

The hours crept along until it was midnight and Victor got up, unfolding his tall frame in a bone-cracking stretch. Brooke rose, too, walking around the room and meandering to the window.

"Fog's rolled back in," she said. "This is sure different from Southern California." Pulling the curtain aside she gazed into the night until she jerked back from the window with a scream that went right through him. He was at her side in a second. She turned into his arms, breath caught and eyes wide with fright. "I saw a man. Out there." She pointed a shaking finger toward the courtyard.

"Stay here, and I mean it this time," he said before racing down the hall and out into the damp air.

The overgrown shrubbery in the outside courtyard threw strange shadows on the pavement. He heard the sound of his own breathing, the wind rustling the leaves. Motionless, he listened for any noise of an intruder but he heard nothing.

Prowling the other side of the small stone wall, he looked for evidence of a man's presence. The grass was flattened in some places, but he could not be sure it was the result of human feet. After another ten minutes of searching, he turned up nothing of interest. Had she imagined it? All the talk of treasure and tunnels, the shooting at his office, worry about her father and her brother, had it preyed on her nerves to the point where the shadows came alive in her imagination?

He trudged back to the dorm, suddenly tired. The euphoria of their earlier discovery was wearing off in the face of this complication. What was he doing chasing after a man she might have dreamed up? Brooke was emotional, spiritual and stubbornly illogical. A dancer, a dreamer surely, to believe they would find a Tarkenton and somehow restore her father's reputation. What was he doing buying into her fanciful notions?

Then again, wasn't he also dreaming, to think this adventure might somehow lead him to his wife's killer? For some reason the anger that perpetually hummed in his veins had quieted the past couple of days. Probably just dulled by the intrigue of finding a treasure. He felt off-balance, prone to a slight disequilibrium he couldn't explain. The thoughts followed him back to the women's dorm.

"I didn't find anyone," he said, stopping so quickly his shoes squeaked on the tile.

Standing between the women was a man he'd never seen before.

"We did," said Stephanie, her voice grim. "Or rather, he found us."

Brooke's heart was still hammering from the stranger's arrival. He was young, not more than mid-twenties, with dark skin and a wild head of springy curls. Dressed in boots, jeans and a sweatshirt, with

Sea World marked in faded letters, he looked as though he might be arriving after working a night shift driving a truck. His eyes glittered appraisingly as he gave them a thorough inspection.

"Who are you?" Victor barked, moving closer.

"Stryker."

"Stryker who?"

He shrugged and moved to the chair, sitting heavily. "Just Stryker."

"What do you want?"

He cocked his head. "You the only one that talks? Chicks aren't allowed?"

Victor took an angry step forward. "Listen."

Brooke jumped in quickly. "Stryker, this part of the campus is closed. Why did you come here?"

"To find you."

"Why?"

"Low on cash. Looking for some employment opportunities."

Victor's eyes narrowed. "And what exactly would we be hiring you to do?"

He stared back at Victor, dark eyes gleaming. "I'm an urban explorer. Anyplace dark, deserted and abandoned, I'm there. I've seen tunnels all over California. Happen to know you're interested in tunnels."

"How did you happen to know that?" Stephanie said.

"Not hard to figure out. Since the campus was emptied, this is the perfect place to explore. Saw you coming out of the dorm the other day with the banged-up dean."

"Saw us? Maybe you had something to do with turning out the lights?"

He shrugged. "I was poking around. Saw you, is all."

"Are you a student here?" Brooke asked.

He laughed. "Nah. I'm an out-of-work cabbie."

"Then how did you know that was the dean?" Victor asked.

"Saw his picture in the paper, right after I moved here. He was talking about a missing professor who worked at the college."

"Do you know anything about that?" Victor said.

He shook his head slowly. "It's not difficult, big man. You have some reason to want to go into those tunnels. I can take you. I've been exploring all over Bayside. I know places."

"Know any places around Gage Library?" said Stephanie, ignoring a warning glance from Victor.

"Maybe. How much is it worth to you?"

"Mr. Stryker, no offense, but you're a complete stranger to us and you let yourself in uninvited. Why would we trust you in any way?"

He shrugged. "Hey, man. I'm just looking to save up some cash to go start over with my girl, some-where warm." His lip curled. "I hate this city. Cold even in the summer and not enough work for cab-bies. I don't figure on staying here long. If you don't want my help—" he held palms up to the ceiling

"—no sweat. I'll find something else, but you're never going to find your way around on your own."

"Why so sure?" Stephanie said. "We might be better than you think."

He gave her an appreciative grin. "Maybe, but down there it's a different world. You could get lost for a long time, a really long time, before somebody found you."

Victor exhaled before he spoke. "Tell you what. Why don't you meet us there at the library tomorrow and if you can show us something, then we'll talk about payment."

"I'll be there." Stryker paused a moment. "Don't mention me to the dean. He's had the security people kick me out before." Stryker helped himself to a bag of chips from the table before he left. Stephanie locked the door behind him.

Brooke squeezed her hands together to stop them from shaking.

Victor laid a hand on her shoulder, fingers grazing her collarbone. "Okay?"

She nodded. "He scared me, is all. Do you think he can really show us more of the tunnels?"

"Maybe, but I don't trust him. I figured we'll let him think we're playing along. That way we can keep tabs on him."

Stephanie laughed. "You don't trust anyone, but in this case you might be right. It is pretty coincidental, him showing up."

"Uh-huh," Victor said, looking out the window.

"Making sure he's leaving?" Brooke said, wishing he hadn't moved his hand away from her shoulder.

Victor nodded. "That, and wondering if he happens to ride a motorcycle."

Brooke endured a restless night even though Victor made sure they locked the door and he personally checked all the doors and windows on the floor before he left. At first light, she eased out of bed and found that Stephanie was already up and packing gear, including more sandwiches and bottled water.

Brooke did some stretches, a habit hammered into her by endless hours of dance training, excused herself to the outer hallway and dialed her phone.

Her father answered on the third ring.

"Dad," she said, relief surging through her at his deep baritone. "I'm so glad to catch you. I called last night, but no one answered."

"Brooke, honey. I've been thinking about you."

She smiled. "I've missed you. Can't wait to come home, hopefully with good news."

"I know you're going to do just fine on those auditions."

The smile died on her lips. "Dad…"

"When you come home, we'll have a party. You can do a little recital to show off."

Her voice failed her as her father prattled on, his mind snared in a time years before when she was living her dream, apprenticing with a dance company in New York, and he was enjoying the lifetime achievement of assistant curator. It was a time before the injury, before she had to drop out, before everything had fallen apart in her life and her father's. She could not find the words to stop him, until the phone clattered to the floor and Denise was suddenly on the line.

"Hi, Brooke. Your father dropped the phone."

"He thinks I'm still at the dance academy," she mumbled.

She sighed. "He's confused. He spent yesterday thinking we were back in our own college days, eating noodles and drinking coffee. It's kinder sometimes, I think, when he's back in happier times. Where are you?"

Brooke filled her in.

She sucked in a breath. "I can hardly believe it. I'm thrilled. And terrified. To think you might actually be close to finding the Tarkenton." Denise could appreciate the idea more than anyone except her father. She, too, had spent years following Donald on the trail of the elusive painting. Her tone changed. "But, honey, it sounds dangerous."

"I'm here with the Gages, and Dean Lock has appointed a guardian to watch over us."

"Don't trust Lock. He's not the man he seems to be."

Brooke was beginning to realize the truth of those words. Nothing was what it seemed to be.

"Why didn't you tell me you and Dad came to visit Colda on your last trip?"

"I thought your father did. It isn't all that important anyway, because we never saw Colda. Your father wanted to talk to him but he wasn't there, so we stayed the night in a hotel and left without seeing him. I even went back to Bayside a second time while your father was sleeping, but I still couldn't find Colda." She paused. "I only discovered during the course of that trip that he'd sent the Tarkenton to Colda in the first place."

Brooke heard the hurt in her aunt's voice. "I didn't know it either."

"It bothered me a lot at first, but his bouts of confusion were becoming more frequent, so I guess we can't take it personally."

Her stomach heaved, cold fear taking hold deep in her gut. *No, Dad. Don't leave me. I need you to be my father.* Her mother had moved on, married again, and Brooke had only awkward conversations with her. She'd never been able to decide if their lack of connection was due to Brooke's anger or her mother's guilt. Didn't matter. Gone was gone, and her father was the priority. She forced herself to focus back on the conversation. "Tell me about that trip."

"I was ready to grill Colda, to make him produce the painting and tell us his opinion right on the spot, but he never showed. Your father wanted to take the painting back, so we went to the professor's apartment." She sighed. "I have to confess, the door was open so we went inside. The place was an absolute mess, but the Tarkenton wasn't there, only a reproduction, an amateur copy that Colda probably did himself, so we went back home. The police contacted us after Colda disappeared and I told them the whole story."

Brooke was surprised to find they'd been so thorough.

Denise went on. "I wondered if your father had gotten confused again, that he hadn't sent the painting to Colda in the first place, maybe he'd just sent along some pictures, until I found a receipt for a delivery service to Colda's address after we got home. I told you about that, didn't I?"

"Yes, that was another reason I came here."

She sighed. "I'm sorry, honey. Half the time I don't know if I'm coming or going around here."

"It's okay. This just makes me think that maybe Colda took off with the painting."

Denise huffed into the phone. "If the work really is a Tarkenton, it would be worth millions. Your father never should have sent it."

Brooke shivered. "I wish he hadn't."

"And I wonder, too... Oh, never mind."

"What?"

"I'm worried about the shooting. Do you think someone is watching you? Believing you'll lead them to Colda and the painting?"

She thought about Stryker, Tuney, the motorcycle chase. The chill of the hallways swept through her. "I'll be all right."

"Be sure you are, honey. A treasure like that can make people do strange things. Call me if you need anything."

"Okay. Talk to you later." Brooke clicked off the phone with fingers suddenly gone cold. Stephanie startled her.

"Phoning home?"

Brooke nodded. "Are we really going to start hunting for treasure in the Gage Library?"

"Yup. Stranger things have happened. I once found a Babe Ruth baseball card in a stolen Bugatti."

"Did you recover the car for a client?"

"Nope. I'm the one who stole it."

Brooke couldn't keep her mouth from dropping open.

"Sorry to shock, but I make it a point now not to cover up my past sins." Stephanie laughed. "My brothers rescued me from a man who was a very bad influence. Don't worry. I'm reformed, mostly reformed anyway. Victor worries still. Let's go."

Brooke had to half jog to keep up with Stephanie's long strides. She thought about Victor, serious and pragmatic, doggedly determined. Stephanie Gage had once stolen a car? How had her brothers rescued her? Outwardly calm and in control, she had a feeling that deep down Victor might be capable of anything when it came to those he loved.

NINE

Victor zipped his jacket against the thick fog, glad to see Brooke had brought one along this time. His backpack was filled with the supplies he imagined they might need, as were those the two women carried. Stephanie checked her cell phone as they headed toward the stately marble steps of Gage Library.

His father was proud of the structure, he knew. There was nothing Wyatt Gage liked better in the world than a library. Even better was a library with the Gage name on the front. Victor looked around for Stryker, but there was no sign of him.

"Maybe Stryker decided he wasn't the treasure trove of information he told us he was," Victor said. "Can't say I'm surprised."

Brooke nodded. "And where's Tuney? Didn't he stay in the men's dorm with you last night?"

"Yes," Victor said. "Snores like a freight train." He looked around. "Should have been right behind me."

Stephanie waved her phone. "Just got a text from him. He'll catch up. He's got something to look into."

Victor's stomach tensed. "I wonder what he's up to."

Dean Lock pulled up in a security cart, hobbling awkwardly toward them, a single crutch propped under his armpit. "I can't see how searching the library will be of much help. It's had workmen crawling all over it for the past four months. If Colda left a painting there, they would have found it."

Victor decided not to tell him about the altered painting in Colda's apartment. For the moment he wanted to start the search quickly. "We'll keep you posted."

Lock shifted. "I would come in with you, but there's a chancellor's meeting at our other location, which I've got to attend, and with this ankle..."

"I'll give you a call later and fill you in on our progress, or Tuney will. He'll be along in a minute. We'll see you later, then." Victor turned to go.

"Just so you know," Lock called. "The police called me." He hesitated. "They may have located Colda."

Brooke's jaw dropped open. "That's wonderful. Where? Can we talk to him?"

Lock held up a hand. "No details yet, but they said they'd call. So there may be no point to your treasure hunting."

"We'll keep looking until they've found Colda and we can ask him personally what happened to the Ramseys' painting." Victor's own words surprised him. So protective of Ms. Ramsey's property now? He could see the thought in the dean's eyes. Turning on his heel, he followed Stephanie and Brooke into the darkened interior of the library.

Groping for the switch, he brushed past Brooke, her hair grazing his cheek. A strong desire to pull her close and bury his face in those silky strands swept through him. In a moment he found the switch, and the cavernous space was thrown into view. All three of them were silent for a moment, taking in the massive dark wood shelves, some empty, some swaddled in a sturdy canvas. The floors were tile, aged and speckled, and windows high up in the peaked ceilings added a strange illumination. In the center of the lofty ceiling was a circular stained glass window that tinted the room in subtle color.

Stephanie whistled. "Daddy did good."

Victor laughed.

Brooke stood in the middle of the massive stacks of books and did a slow circle. "Incredible."

Her face tipped upward, lips parted in awe. Incredible, he agreed.

She shook her head after a moment. "If the police found Colda, then what are we really doing here?"

"Never stake your treasure on 'ifs,'" Stephanie said. "As Luca says, it's not over until the smoke clears."

Brooke's laugh spiraled up toward the arched roof, mingling with another sound.

Victor froze. "Did you hear that?"

Both Stephanie and Brooke shook their heads.

"It was a noise, from the upper level."

"Might be a rat that got in." She sneezed. "This place hasn't been used in a while."

Victor knew she was probably right. Rats. Nothing more.

"I say we poke around in the out-of-the-way cracks and crevices. I'll start in the back. You two take the wings on the left and right," Stephanie directed.

"Stay with us," Victor called. "Safer."

Stephanie's grin said it all. "Since when have I gone for safety?"

Victor sighed. "Text me in ten minutes, or I'm coming to find you."

"Yes, big brother," she called with a laugh.

He found Brooke looking at him, a gentle smile on her face. "You take good care of your sister."

"I try to, but it's like herding cats."

"She, er, mentioned she'd appropriated a car."

Victor exhaled. "She...lost someone important to her and went a little wild. That's history." History that left deeply buried scars on both of them.

He led Brooke down the first wing, which housed a collection of something that had been removed. The empty shelves were covered by a layer of dust. Construction equipment dotted the long hallway.

He listened for the strange noise he'd heard earlier, but there was nothing but the sound of their feet moving across the tiled floor.

Just the circumstances playing with his mind.

They saw nothing out of place in the long corridor.

"How about there?" Brooke said, her whisper tingling his ear.

She pointed to an unobtrusive door marked Tech Room A-6. They passed into a room filled with wood tables and a bank of countertops that probably housed a row of computers.

"Brings back memories of med school," he said.

"Hours of studying?"

He nodded. "I didn't mind. Books are a lot easier to read than people."

Her lips curled into that wide, open smile that struck a chord somewhere deep inside him. "That's what gets me into trouble," she said. "I always think people are what they portray themselves to be." Her smile faltered. "Dumb."

He wanted to comfort, to soothe, but he could not think of the right words. Instead he cupped her cheek with his hand, hoping the warmth in his fingertips would bring back the smile to her face. She leaned into this touch, her face molding perfectly into his palm.

A buzzing of his cell made him pull his hand away. "Stephanie's okay. Wants us to come to the second floor pronto."

They scurried along the deserted hallway without speaking, giving Victor time to think. Why had he touched her? Why had the feel of her satin cheek given him a warm sensation in the place where his heart used to be?

He quickened his pace until they reached the staircase and they jogged up into the dark second floor. They were greeted by a labyrinth of shelves covered in plastic with boxes of books stacked on top. Above them catwalks spanned the space and drew the eye up to the glass skylight, which revealed the swirling fog outside.

A faint light shone from the back, almost obliterated by the dark shadows cast by the bookshelves.

"This way," Victor said, taking her hand.

They started down a narrow aisle. He stopped, again thinking he had heard a noise.

Brooke opened her mouth to respond when something scuffled over their heads. Victor had only a split second to react. He yanked her toward him as a stack of loaded boxes crashed down into the space where Brooke had been standing only a moment before.

Her body fell on his and he wrapped his arms around her as the contents of the boxes, massive leather-bound tomes, burst from the containers, slamming into Brooke's back in spite of his sheltering embrace. He could feel the impact push the air out of her. She cried out as he tried to fend off the falling books.

In another second, Stephanie was there, pulling books away, helping them both to their feet. "I saw someone, a man I think, but he was running for the stairs. You okay?"

Much to Victor's relief Brooke made it to her feet,

a dazed look on her face. "I think so." They both turned their attention to Victor as he sat up.

"I'm okay, too, just banged up a little. What did the guy look like?"

"I don't know," Stephanie said. "I only saw a shadow, really, which I assumed was a man. Could have been a woman, I suppose."

"We should get out of here," Victor said.

Brooke shook her head. "No. This just proves that we're on the right track."

"It also proves you're not safe."

"I'm fine." She shook herself and rubbed at one shoulder. "It was just some old books."

Victor picked up one of the hefty volumes. "Old and heavy. Could have delivered a significant injury. The safest idea is to get out of here. Come back with some cops, maybe, if we can get any of them to believe us."

"No one is leaving here," Stephanie said, her eyes gleaming, "until you see what I found."

In spite of her bravado, Brooke's legs were still shaky as she followed Stephanie into the darkness. Her shoulder throbbed from the impact of a book slamming into it. She could still feel Victor's arms around her, holding him to her chest, shielding her body with his.

He's just here to convict your father, she reminded herself. *Don't paint his motives in any other way.*

She tried to make sense of the whole situation as

they followed Stephanie. Was Colda missing or not? Why had he dodged a meeting with her father? And missed his flight? Who didn't want them to find the answers? The confusion in her mind worried her more than the circumstances. Was her father's devastating genetic legacy playing out in her, too? Both her father's illness and her brother's were caused by a mutation of the same gene, though with completely different results. Tad's full mutation left him a child, mentally. Her father's permutation of the same gene gave him a normal life until recently. Was there a ticking time bomb in her genes, too? She knew female symptoms of FXTAS were milder, but she couldn't help wondering.

She shuddered, and Victor put a hand on her shoulder.

"Okay?"

She straightened, willing her body to stop trembling. Tall and straight like the dancer she used to be. "Yes," she said as they turned into a room that was no bigger than the small dorm where she and Stephanie bunked. It was crowded with cardboard boxes, crates of yellowed papers and old framed photographs.

"It's a miscellaneous collection of odds and ends," Stephanie said, "but look at this."

She picked up one of the long cardboard tubes and slid out the contents, using the top of a box as a makeshift table. The papers were old and brittle, faded in some places and water-stained in others.

Brooke peered at the document. "Blueprints of…"

"The tunnel system," Victor finished, his voice jubilant. "It dates back to 1932."

Stephanie nodded. "Much of it is probably not relevant anymore after the fire and all the remodeling over the years, but it does show one important thing." She pointed to a tiny detailed image. "It's the library."

"And there's a tunnel entrance from the basement." Brooke had to stop herself from squealing. "I can't believe it. I don't even think the dean knows about this."

"So tell me, sis," Victor said, raising an eyebrow. "How did you know to look in that tube? With all this junk around, why that one?"

She smiled, a cat-got-the-canary grin. "It was missing a top and there were greasy fingerprints on the side."

"Disgusting," Victor said.

"But effective," Brooke added. "We might as well check it out while we're here."

The elevators were not operational so they took the stairs, arriving in a massive space, bisected by neatly wrapped paintings and long rows of filing drawers.

"According to this map, there's an entrance on the northwestern wall."

The electric lights did not fully illuminate the space, which smelled of mold and disuse. Brooke's heart beat fast with an excitement she had not felt since she was a part of a dance company. Could they really be inches away from a tunnel that hid her father's priceless Tarkenton?

She moved ahead of the others, straining against the darkness to find the outline of a door, or some rusted sign that might point the way. Try as she might, she saw no sign of any such thing, only a solid row of file cabinets standing like soldiers against the walls. Pushing into the darkness, she stopped so suddenly Victor plowed into her from behind.

"What is it?"

"Feel."

She took his hand and moved it to the level of her face.

"Cool air."

"Yes."

Victor moved closer to the wall, feeling for the draft. "It's coming from behind these file cabinets. Move back and I'll ease one out."

Brooke pulled back into the darkness, the thrill of discovery pushing away her earlier worries. Stephanie held up a flashlight to help Victor maneuver. The drawers must have been filled because Victor strained, arms tensed as he wrestled the awkward bundle.

She moved back another few steps to give him more room when a hand came out of the darkness and clamped onto her shoulder.

She screamed.

Stephanie whirled the flashlight around and Victor

let go of the filing cabinet so abruptly it toppled forward with a crash.

Tuney stared at them, wide-eyed. "Care to explain why you're burgling university property?"

"You first," Victor said, breathing hard. "Where have you been?"

"Just like I texted. Looking into some things. That's what I'm paid to do. Took me a while to find you. So?" He pointed to the file cabinet. "Explanations?"

"Help me move it and you'll see for yourself."

Brooke exchanged a look with Stephanie as the two men heaved the file cabinet out of the way.

"Bring the light closer, Steph."

Stephanie shone her flashlight directly on the wall previously covered by the file drawers.

"There," Brooke said, excitement swelling inside. "You can see the outline. It's a door."

"No lock that I can see," Victor said, pulling a penknife from his pocket and wedging it in the crack. It didn't budge. Brooke noticed a small depression in the bottom edge, almost at floor level. "It's meant to roll up."

Victor stuck his fingers in the slot and heaved. Slowly, with a sound like a groan of pain, the door inched upward until Tuney had enough room to grab the bottom and add his strength. The door crept up and the four of them peered inside.

"I didn't see that coming," Stephanie said.

"Me, neither." Victor wiped his hands. "It goes

straight down." He beamed his flashlight into the pitch-black shaft.

Brooke could just make out the shape of a rusty ladder, the lower parts lost in the darkness. "Does it go down to the tunnels?"

Tuney snorted. "Probably just leads to another collapsed passage. That ladder looks like it hasn't been used for a couple of decades. It's gonna collapse, and whoever is on it is going straight to the bottom."

Stephanie leaned into the space and Victor grabbed her waist as she played the light closely over the ladder. "Looks sound enough. The rust is rubbed away in some places, maybe from a person's feet."

"Conjecture," Tuney said.

"What's the matter?" Stephanie said as she straightened. "Afraid of ladders?"

"No." Tuney rolled his shoulders and Brooke saw the bead of sweat on his face. "Not so keen about closed-in places. This basement is bad enough."

Brooke felt sorry for him, but she knew there was no way she would be discouraged from going down that ladder. "Why don't you stay here?" she suggested. "You can call for help if we get into trouble."

Tuney's face was grim. "I'm coming. Might as well die falling off a ladder as any other way."

Victor caught Brooke's arm as she started to move past him. "Not a bad idea, about someone staying behind."

"Would you?" she asked.

Face sober, eyes inscrutable in the weak light, he

shook his head. "No, but I'm not always known for practicing restraint either."

"My father's only chance might be down there," she said. "So right now I'm not worrying about restraint."

Was it her imagination or did his hand linger on hers before he nodded and stepped away? Brooke saw Stephanie eyeing her with an odd expression.

Maybe it hadn't been her imagination after all.

Ignoring the tickle in her spine, she took the headlamp Victor held out to her and made her way to the edge.

TEN

Victor snapped on his headlamp and lowered himself onto the rungs, ignoring the discontented sigh from his sister. "I'm heavier," he explained again. "If the ladder is going to give way, we might as well find out about it sooner rather than later."

The steel was cold under his fingers and slightly damp. It was what Victor imagined a sewer tunnel was like, only there was no bad smell, only the slight funk of moisture and a tang of metal. When he made it down fifteen or so rungs, he heard Brooke start down, then Stephanie, who had finished explaining to an incredulous Tuney a few select details about the clues in the doctored painting.

The scuffling of their feet echoed wildly in the long tube.

"Can't see Colda poking around in the dark," Tuney called, and Victor thought he caught suppressed tension in the man's voice.

"Why not?" Stephanie said. "His students said he was perpetually curious, more interested in the campus and art history than his teaching duties."

Victor called them to a stop. "Listen."

They clung there, headlamps throwing the light around as they strained to see.

"Sounds like something moving," Brooke whispered. "Down below."

They listened for another moment until the sound stopped.

"An animal?" Stephanie suggested.

Victor didn't reply. It wasn't an animal that worried him. It was the man on the motorcycle, the one who might have killed a woman in the lobby or toppled the box of books from the catwalk. He didn't even bother to try to discourage the others from continuing. The only one who might listen was Tuney, judging from his panicky breathing, but his stubborn streak was wide enough to keep him on the ladder.

Instead he continued on, holding each damp rung securely. Another four feet, and the temperature began to climb. It warmed to the point where he found himself stopping to unzip his jacket with one hand. The smell changed, too—now a hint of fetid stink tainted the air.

Without much warning the ladder ended and Victor dismounted onto a dry floor. He could not see the dimensions of the room at first as he assisted the others off the ladder.

Brooke flipped on a handheld flashlight. They were in a circular cement room with three openings leading out. None of them bore any kind of signage or a hint that they had been traveled anytime in the last hundred years.

Stephanie unrolled the map and peered at it with a penlight. "Map shows three tunnels, all right, but it's unclear where they emerge."

Brooke peered into each one. "Can't see a thing."

Tuney wiped a hand across his brow. "This is crazy. I'm not going into any of those. Leads to nothing but broken-down equipment. Colda never would have left a painting down here. Guy was an art nut. Putting it in this place would be like setting a match to it."

Brooke sighed. "He's probably right. Without temperature controls and the proper protection, it would be ruined quickly."

"Unless he didn't intend to keep it here long," Victor mused.

Brooke caught his eye. "As in he might have meant to come back for it?"

Victor nodded. "He was spooked by something, too spooked to meet with your father and aunt. He might have stashed it down here and figured on getting it that night or soon thereafter but…"

She finished slowly. "He never got the chance?"

Stephanie said, "If the police really do have a lead about his whereabouts, they can get the whole story."

"But as it stands," Tuney snapped, "we have no proof at all that Colda even set foot in this tunnel."

Victor turned a slow circle, beaming his own light carefully on each of the passageways. Something caught his eye and he stopped, moved closer. Then he laughed.

All three looked at him as though he had lost his mind. "I think that we do have proof that Colda was here."

"You're crazy," Tuney said. "What kind of proof could there be?"

Victor pointed to a small figure, no more than three inches high, drawn in permanent marker on the cement next to the farthest-right passage.

They crowded close to see.

"I don't believe it," Stephanie said. "The old professor is really something."

"He certainly is," Victor said, watching Tuney's face as he saw the drawing of the little black pawn.

Tuney shook his head. "This doesn't make sense."

"Nope," Brooke said cheerfully. "None of it does, but we know that Colda has been here and left a marker for himself."

"Good enough for me," Stephanie said, shouldering her pack. "Let's go."

Victor checked the time on his luminous watch.

Stephanie perused the map she'd borrowed from the room upstairs. "I don't understand these markings. There are three squares scattered throughout the tunnel work but there's no indication of what the squares represent."

"Pumping stations, maybe?" Victor suggested.

Brooke nodded, and he could see the glitter of

excitement in her eyes and knew his must reveal the same.

"This could actually be it," she said, her voice hushed. "We could be close to finding my father's Tarkenton."

Or not, he thought. *We could be one step closer to finding out your father had something to do with Colda's disappearance. Or that Donald stole the painting from someone else and had to cover his tracks.* If Donald was a thief, then there was every reason to believe he'd arranged for the theft four years prior and hired the thug who crashed into Jennifer's car.

Then I'll prove it.

I have to.

For Jennifer.

He looked into the endless hole before them, with the strange feeling that the world would be different when they emerged back into the light.

If he believed, if he could bend his heart to the faith that warmed Jennifer and seemed to sustain Brooke, he would pray for...what?

Vengeance, at long last?

Or something else?

He stepped toward the pitch-black passage.

Brooke felt as if she was being swallowed alive by the darkness as she followed Victor in. Their headlamps made small inroads, illuminating the curved walls that stretched before them. Pipes of various sizes snaked along the ceiling, dotted here and there with cobwebs.

Victor stopped every ten feet to spray a small arrow with his can of glow-in-the-dark paint. The arrows pointed the way out. Small comfort as they followed the passage along. The air was still warm, the floor dry, which encouraged Brooke.

Victor brought them suddenly to a halt when the tunnel split off in two. "Right or left?"

They looked closely, but it was Tuney who spotted the hand-drawn chess piece. "Left," he said, jabbing a finger toward the pawn.

As the moved along, Brooke felt the hair rise on the back of her neck. She stopped and looked around, shining her light into the dark crevices of the tunnel.

"See something?" Tuney said, voice tense.

"I guess not."

They continued on until she felt it again, a faint stirring in the air, or perhaps her imagination. *There's nothing here that can hurt me,* she thought, and whispered a prayer for courage.

Stephanie edged next to her, reaching up to tap on the metal beams above their heads. "These things haven't been tended to in decades."

Brooke looked above at the cracks running through the surface. "Looks like stone up there."

Tuney suddenly turned. "I heard it. A groaning sound. You don't think…?"

Victor turned his light into the tunnel ahead and they all saw reflected back at them a dozen sets of eyes. Then the rats were upon them, skittering over the pipes, rushing along the floor in a moving pack.

Brooke screamed and jerked back, as did Stephanie. Victor pressed through the furry bodies and joined them, flattening himself against the wall as best he could. "Something scared them," he yelled over the noise.

Tuney leaped up onto one of the pipes that jutted from above and hung there, monkeylike, as the rats continued to course by, pattering across his fingers. Over the sound of their nails whisking over the floor came a louder noise as the tunnel seemed to groan around them.

"It's coming down," Victor yelled.

The ceiling was trembling now, bits of rock flying through the air. Tuney hung there in the tumult, his face frozen in shock, until the heavy piping began to tear loose from the ceiling.

With it came an enormous chunk of stone that crashed down, scattering the rats and shaking the tunnel around them.

Tuney dropped and rolled.

Brooke temporarily lost sight of him as she tried to stay upright against the trembling that threatened to knock her over. A choking cloud of dust enveloped her.

She felt Victor grabbing her hand in a death grip and then she was being hauled farther down the tunnel. "Come on," he shouted. "This way."

They ran as best they could, the floor rocking

underneath them. A piece of rock flew into Brooke's face, cutting her cheek. She fought to stay upright as they ran over a floor littered with debris before they made it to a tunnel that branched off from the main. Victor pulled Brooke and Stephanie close to the wall. Brooke found herself pressed in, her face touching the warm skin of Victor's neck. She heard the breath shuddering through him, felt the taut muscles in his neck and chest. The sound of collapse grew so loud she thought her eardrums would explode.

All at once it stopped, gradually petering away until there was only the slight trickling of rock fragments and then nothing at all. Dust thick as ash swirled through the air.

The silence was almost more terrifying than the noise. Victor lifted her chin. "All right?" he asked.

She nodded, numbed by the close call and the gentle way his thumb reached up to stroke her chin, wiping away some of the dust. He turned to make sure Stephanie was unhurt.

Stephanie nodded at Victor. "That was exciting."

"Tuney's weight on the pipe must have caused a collapse," Victor said.

They came to the realization at the same moment. "Where's Tuney?" Brooke whispered, her heart constricting. Victor took off back toward the main tunnel and she followed him, heart pounding in her throat.

"Lord, please," she breathed as she ran, nameless dread coursing through her veins. He was her enemy, bent on destroying her father, but she did not want to find him broken and bleeding.

Victor stopped short at the connection to the main tunnel. The entrance was completely obscured by a tangle of fallen pipes and chunks of debris. "Tuney," he yelled.

There was no answer.

All three of them began to yell until their voices echoed wildly through the dust swirled air.

"Quit yelling," came the faint reply. "I'm going deaf."

"Tuney," Brooke cried. "You're okay?"

"Banged up, and I don't see any way to get to where you are."

Victor tried to dig away at the debris but the effort only caused more shifting in the towering mass. He wiped a filthy hand over his face. "Can you get back out?"

After a moment, Tuney grumbled his answer. "Yeah. Think I can see your glow marks. Can't get any cell coverage down here so I'll have to go get help."

"You sure you'll be all right?" Brooke said.

"What choice do I have? I followed you crazy people down here and now I've got to get you out or let you all die down here with the rats. I told you this was a ridiculous idea."

Brooke, Stephanie and Victor exchanged smiles. Tuney's stream of complaints grew fainter as he moved away. "And I told them I didn't like dark places. See what happens in dark places? Things fall on you, and there are rats. Bucket loads of 'em."

Victor exhaled. "At least he seems unharmed, judging by the complaining."

Stephanie beamed her flashlight around. "And at least the rats have gone."

Brooke shivered, remembering the feel of the rats brushing the top of her head. "What caused them to run?"

"Maybe they felt an earthquake?"

"Did we disturb them with our movements?" Stephanie asked.

Victor looked thoughtful. "I'm not sure."

They were in a short section of tunnel, a tight cube of pipes occupying one corner. The far end was blocked by a metal grate, similar to the one they'd seen in the basement of the women's dorm. Victor's tug revealed the lock was sound, the metal bars that crisscrossed the opening too sturdy to break through.

Brooke felt a tingle of panic. "Looks like we're trapped here."

"Only until Tuney gets out," Stephanie said.

"He'll get out, won't he?" Brooke asked.

Victor nodded. "He'll find a way. He's tenacious."

Stephanie sat down on the floor and crossed her legs. Her face was sweat-streaked, a coating of dirt marring the normal shine of her dark hair. "Still, if he doesn't, it could pose a problem."

Brooke put the pieces together. "Because no one

knows about the tunnel map except the three of us. So even if Lock sent a rescue team to find us…"

"There's no guarantee they'd make it anytime soon," Victor said. "And I wonder…"

"What?"

"For some reason Lock doesn't want us in these tunnels in the first place."

"But he wouldn't leave us here," Brooke said in horror. "He wouldn't."

Victor's eyes were flat and cold as stone when he answered. "Wouldn't he?"

Brooke had no answer. She could not bring herself to believe Lock would abandon them to die. "I can't accept that."

Victor's face softened as he looked at her. "I'm not used to seeing the good side of people. I'm sure you're right."

Brooke wanted to touch him then, to bring the tenderness back to his face that she had seen before. Had he always been so hardened about his fellow man? Or was that a consequence of his wife's violent death? She was distracted from her thoughts by Stephanie.

"Guys, Lock may not be our biggest problem right now."

Victor gave her a questioning glance.

"The temperature," she explained. "It's rising. Rapidly."

ELEVEN

Victor was amazed he hadn't noticed the change himself. The temperature was definitely hot and seemed to be edging up with every passing second. He took off his jacket, sweat already dampening his shirt. "This must vent from an active steam tunnel."

"Active?" Stephanie said. "I thought the tunnels were shut down due to the renovation."

He shrugged. "Guess they haven't gotten around to shutting them all down yet."

Brooke's face was flushed, cheeks pink.

Stephanie fanned her sweaty bangs with a notepad. "Probably close to eighty in here already, and climbing."

Victor studied the walls again, which were comprised of rows of neatly constructed brickwork with no exit to be seen. He shined his flashlight through the locked grate again, trying to decide if the air felt cooler on the other side. He looked around for a section of pipe or rock, anything that he could use to hammer at the lock.

Brooke understood and peered around. "Here," she said triumphantly. "I found a loose brick in the debris."

He hammered at the sturdy lock, hitting it so hard that sparks flew through the darkness. The brick only seemed to ding and scratch the lock, which showed no signs of weakening. No shoddy construction here. He kept at it anyway, frustration fueling his efforts in spite of the heat that now seemed to press down on him from all sides.

The doctor side of his brain took over.

Hyperthermia would be the result of prolonged exposure to excessive heat. When their bodies became too overwhelmed to self-regulate, their temperatures would climb uncontrollably. And when they soared into the neighborhood of 104, they would all be in danger of heatstroke. He looked at Brooke. Was she acting confused? Dizzy? Was Stephanie's face still damp with sweat or becoming hot and dry, a sure sign that she was succumbing?

"Drink as much water as you can," he called to them, pounding harder, harder, willing the lock to give way.

"Stop, Victor." Brooke held on to his arm. "It's not going to help. You're going to overheat yourself faster."

"I can't just sit here."

"Maybe the temperature will stabilize," Brooke said.

"Or maybe it won't."

"Stephanie is trying her phone again. Please, Victor." Her tone was pleading now.

Stephanie's slow shake of the head told him that wasn't going to work. His hands burned from the effort of pounding. Sweat streamed off his face.

"Victor," Brooke said, tugging at his arm. "You've got to stop."

He turned on her. "I'm not going to sit by and watch two more women die."

"We'll be all right," Brooke said.

"You don't know that. No one can know that." Anger spiraled inside him.

She looked at him with a calm that made his rage boil over.

"What do you suggest? Prayer? If you're so tight with God, why don't you offer up a prayer now and see if He could help us out?"

She looked down.

"What's the matter?" he said, feeling the same fury he'd felt after Jennifer died. "Are you afraid He isn't listening?"

"No."

"What is it, then?" Victor demanded, body on fire.

She lifted her head then and transfixed him with such a penetrating look, soft and gentle, that it momentarily doused his anger. "He always listens," she said. "But sometimes He says no."

He turned away then, trying to collect the thoughts that rose up inside him like a flame. How could she have that soft gentleness about her? How could it survive the bashing and humiliation, the fear that he knew she must have about inheriting the family disease?

"I won't accept it. I won't let anything else be taken from me," he barked as he started hammering away again until his vision started to blur.

Brooke made a move to stop him, but Stephanie called to her. "Come sit with me. We'll look at the map and see if there's anything we might have missed."

They sank to the floor and he shot them a quick look. Red faced, eyes wide.

Soon they would become unresponsive.

Then they would stop breathing, stepping over the void into a place from which he could not bring them back, like he hadn't been able to bring Jennifer back.

He pounded until his hands bled.

His peripheral vision failed and all he could see was that unyielding metal before him.

Hotter and hotter.

So hot he felt as if he was being cooked.

Sweat poured down his face.

The futility of his labors became clear when the brick broke in his hands and the lock remained fast.

His eyes found Stephanie's through the gloom. He saw that she understood.

He could not get them out.

His head dropped and he felt the strength ooze out of him until he could barely stand. An arm went around his waist and Brooke was there, gently moving him away, urging him to sit next to her.

"It's okay," she said. "We'll wait here for Tuney. You did your best."

"My best wasn't enough. Not for Pearson, Jackney and Rivera." *And not for Jennifer.*

"Who are they, Victor?"

He could not answer. He could not manage to draw a full breath. His body had overheated to the point of no return.

"Sorry," he whispered.

She wiped his face with the sleeve of her jacket and pressed a water bottle to his lips. "Drink."

He didn't want to soothe the fire in his body to accept the comfort of her touch on his face. The only thing that could quench the heat was the knowledge that Stephanie and Brooke would not die in that dark hole. Just as he summoned up his last remaining bit of strength to try to stand again, a grinding noise filled the space.

Brooke looked wildly around. "What's that?"

"It's coming from behind the pipes," Stephanie whispered.

Victor tried to ease the flashlight out of his pocket. Who or what was making the noise? His body refused to cooperate. He could not force his shaking hands to act.

Just before he passed out, Victor thought he heard a voice, a man's voice, but he knew it couldn't be.

He let the darkness claim him.

* * *

Brooke froze from her position on her knees, wetting Victor's forehead as she saw a stone panel in the floor ease away. A head appeared in the opening, a head bristling with braids.

"Stryker," she cried out, body shuddering with relief. She knew Victor would not make it much longer after his superhuman effort to free them.

He heaved himself up into the space. "Hot in here."

"Where have you been?" Stephanie demanded.

"Seems like we should talk about that later. He don't look so good." He jutted a chin at the unconscious Victor. "Come on."

Without another word he disappeared back into the floor, leaving Brooke and Stephanie to drag Victor to the hole. The air coming from the opening was blessedly cooler and Victor's eyes flickered open. He immediately struggled to get to his feet but both women restrained him.

"Give yourself a minute," Stephanie said, her face washed in relief.

"I'm okay," he said, pushing himself up and grabbing on to a pipe for support, quickly pulling his hand away from the heated metal. "Am I hallucinating or is that a hole in the floor?"

Stryker popped up. "You people are slow."

Victor's eyes widened. "How did he…?"

"We'll sort that out later." Stephanie climbed down a ladder cemented to the side of the passage. "Careful, Victor."

Victor insisted that Brooke go next in spite of her protests. "I'm not leaving until you do."

Brooke saw the futility of arguing and started down twenty feet of ladder, the air growing cooler with each step. Her body shook with the change in temperature, and she wished she could put her jacket on. She stopped to listen for the regular sound of Victor's feet on the rungs above her. His voice reassured her, strong and clear in the darkness.

"I'm fine," he called. "Keep going."

It seemed like forever, though it was probably only a quarter hour or so before they reached the bottom, feet splashing down into several inches of murky water. The chamber they now found themselves in was narrow, low and cool. Both Stryker and Victor had to hunch over.

Stryker pointed. "'Nother hour that way. It's not a direct route but you guys destroyed the other way."

"How did you know that?" Victor said.

"I was hanging back, letting you get a head start." He grinned. "Heard the whole thing so I used another way."

"I thought you were going to be our guide," Stephanie said, brushing a cobweb from her shoulder.

"Looks like I am," Stryker said.

"Why did you stay back?" Brooke prodded.

Stryker scratched his chin. "Saw the dean on the steps of the library. An old guy hanging out with you, too. Didn't feel the need to introduce myself to the whole gang." He rolled his shoulders. "Who's grandpa anyway?"

Brooke watched for Stryker's reaction when she told him. "He's a private investigator hired by the university to find Professor Colda."

Stryker didn't answer.

"Do you know where Colda is?" Brooke asked.

"Nah," Stryker said. "Why would I?"

"Because Professor Colda knew the tunnels well, and so do you," Victor chimed in. "Never came across him in your wanderings?"

"I said no, didn't I? You want to head back or stay here until midnight?" He didn't wait for an answer but splashed away into the tunnel.

They followed, water soaking into their pant legs. Brooke was now cold through and through, but some of the sensation was not physical. Stryker was hiding something. Naïve as she was and blindly trusting as she knew she could be, it was clear that Stryker was not a man to be taken at face value.

Victor felt the same way, she knew.

She saw him check his watch.

"Tuney should have reached the entrance by now, unless it was obstructed," Victor said.

The water grew deeper, now flowing around their knees. Bits of debris swirled around and occasionally something bumped against Brooke's shins, startling her. The flow grew stronger and they had to push against the current. Fatigue began to overwhelm Brooke as she doggedly pressed on.

Victor squeezed by and took her hand, helping her plow through. There was such strength in his touch, even after their recent close call. She thought about his strange comment.

My best wasn't good enough, not for Pearson, Jackney and Rivera.

She understood, or thought she did, about Jennifer, but she did not understand the others. What would it be like to be so alone? To have to carry the responsibility for those around you on your shoulders instead of placing them in God's hands?

God was the only way she got through the day, knowing Tad was living away from his beloved home, watching her father slip deeper into a dark abyss, recalling her ruined dreams of becoming a dancer.

If she believed this world was all there was...

The gloom pressed down, chilling every part of her except her hand, clasped firmly in Victor's. She squeezed his fingers.

He looked at her, surprised. "What's that for?"

"Just wanted to remind you you're not alone."

His mouth opened, but no words came out. After a moment he looked away. "Thanks."

Perhaps it had been too much, too intimate a gesture. When they stopped at the junction of two passageways, the flow of water eased and he let go of her hand, confirming her thoughts.

Ahead was an opening halfway up the wall, approximately five feet by five feet. Stryker pointed them away. "That way."

Victor sloshed forward and peered into the opening. "What's in there?"

"Old utility room. Let's move."

Victor looked over the ledge and peered into the space. "Looks dry in there."

"If you stay here to sightsee, you'll do it alone," Stryker snapped, moving ahead.

"Okay," Victor said, his expression mild. He took out the spray can from his pocket and added an arrow to the wall. "Just in case we want to come back and revisit this location."

Stryker's face was grim, but he did not respond before he marched forward.

Victor lagged back a pace and Brooke saw the excitement on his face. "Tell me."

"I thought I saw some supplies, recent."

"What kind of supplies?"

He was about to answer when Stryker shouted from the front. "Pick up the pace. The water's deepening up here."

Victor pressed his mouth to her ear. "Tell you later."

His lips left a tingling trail down her cheek and neck as they hurried to catch up with Stephanie and Stryker, Victor stopping every so often to spray an arrow on the wall.

It was another hour before they reached another

tiny circular chamber with a sturdy iron ladder leading upward.

Stephanie laughed. "I've had my fill of step aerobics today, but I guess one more won't hurt."

Brooke noticed a series of small metal grates, about a foot square, circling the chamber at intervals. The air coming from them was warm, reminding her of their brush with hyperthermia.

Stryker waited behind, ushering them up the ladder ahead of him. "Leads to an exit just outside the Professor House," he said. "Meet you up top."

Brooke followed Stephanie up, craning her neck to see some glimpse of sky or stars or even the fog that she had so recently grumbled about.

As she climbed past the small grate, legs heavy with fatigue, she felt a prickle across the back of her neck. It was the barest gleam, a speck of white in the darkness, showing for a split second from behind the grate.

A gleam that her overtired senses interpreted in the strangest way.

A set of eyes.

Watching.

From behind the iron bars.

She blinked, and they were gone.

TWELVE

Pushing a heavy round grate aside, they emerged from the tunnel into a darkening courtyard. Victor sucked in a lungful of clean air, delicious after the stale environment in the tunnels. It took him a second to get his bearings and realize that Stryker was right. They were in the rear of the Professor House, the opening tucked neatly behind a clump of overgrown shrubbery that made it nearly invisible to any casual passersby.

He was not surprised to see that Stryker had not emerged from the tunnels.

"Is he okay?" Brooke said, peering back down into the space while Victor replaced the grate. "I don't see any sign of him."

"I'm sure he's fine. Chances are he's the one who left his gear in that room I saw. He's probably living down there."

"But you want to check it out again?"

He nodded. "There's something there that seemed odd but I couldn't put my finger on it and Stryker certainly didn't want us to investigate." He noticed an odd look on Brooke's face. "Something wrong?"

"I… No. All that creeping around is making me paranoid."

"Do you think Stryker will show up tomorrow?" Stephanie said.

Victor considered. "Maybe. He still hasn't gotten any money out of the deal."

Brooke sighed. "This whole thing just keeps getting more complicated."

"I'll second that," Tuney said, emerging from the Professor House. "Just got here and I went inside to use the phone when you all popped out of the ground like a pack of gophers. What happened?"

"Stryker showed us another way out." Victor saw Tuney's eyes search the darkness. "He didn't want to stick around."

"Sounds like an upstanding guy." Tuney scowled as they walked back to the women's dormitory. He checked his phone on the way, listening intently to a voice-mail message.

Victor tried to put the events in order in his mind, to gain some sort of clarity about their next attempt. Should they even try to access the tunnels again? To risk another collapse again for the sliver of a chance that Brooke's theory was correct?

More than a sliver. The painted pawns proved Colda had been down there.

But they didn't prove he'd stashed a Tarkenton there, Victor reminded himself grimly. "I think we've had enough excitement for one day. Let's start again tomorrow."

When they reached the dorm, Tuney excused himself. "I'll be busy tomorrow. Don't suppose it would do any good to tell you three to stay out of trouble until I get back?"

"Probably not," Stephanie said.

Victor noticed the worry lines around Tuney's face, deeper than they had been before. "Is there anything you need to tell us?"

He raised a thick eyebrow. "No."

"Sure?" Victor pressed.

"Yeah." He turned and marched away into the darkness.

Victor walked the ladies to their room and again did his security check of the building. "All locked up tight, but leave your cell phones on anyway."

Victor saw a trickle of fear in Brooke's face. "So what's the plan for tomorrow?"

Was she afraid he would call it off? Or that he wouldn't? His mind wandered back to his earlier outburst. So out of control. So not Victor Gage. He cleared his throat. "I want to study the map again, to return to the chamber we passed, since the original library tunnel is impassable now."

Brooke's brow furrowed. "Do you think there's any way to bypass it?"

"If Stryker can get around those tunnels, then so can we, even if he proves uncooperative. Stephanie is going to do some digging and see if Stryker is just the urban explorer he claims to be."

"You think he's hiding something?"

Victor shrugged. "Seems like pretty coincidental timing, him showing up at the same time we did."

Brooke walked him to the main door, hesitating as if there was something she wanted to say. He studied her face, tired and concerned, wondering how much he'd hurt her by his earlier behavior.

He cleared his throat. "What I said back there, about praying and all that..." He studied the floor. "I apologize."

"No need. You were frustrated."

"But it was wrong to attack you about your beliefs."

She tilted her head. "Your wife was a believer, wasn't she?"

He shifted. "Yes. She tried to share it with me, but I never opened up to it."

"I'm sorry."

"Sometimes, I am, too."

Brooke's eyes shone. "She knew where she was going," she murmured. "She knew where she was going, ultimately, I mean."

He stared at her. *She knew where she was going.*

But she'd left him behind.

Alone.

He wanted to leave the dorm, to escape the strange swirl of emotions that Brooke awakened in him, but she stopped him. "Maybe I spoke out of turn. I'm sorry. It's just something I told my brother when his friend died. He kept asking why. Over and over until I thought my heart would break. Our pastor told him the *why* wasn't as important as the *where*."

"I'm the kind of person who has to know the *why*. I don't blindly trust that God knows all the reasons." He regretted his disdainful tone.

She laughed softly. "Faith isn't blind. Faith is believing, when you can see all around you the reasons to doubt." A bird flew up to the rafters above their heads. "Who are Pearson, Jackney and Rivera? The names you mentioned back there?"

He wanted to tell her, to spill out the burden that weighed so heavily upon him. Looking into those eyes, shining up at him, he could not do it. "I'm really tired. Maybe we can talk another time."

She heard it for what it was, a dismissal. "Of course."

He said good-night, desperate to put some distance between them.

"Victor," she started, a hand half-raised.

"Yes?"

"Back in the tunnel, I—I thought I saw something, as we climbed out."

"What?"

"It's going to sound crazy."

He smiled. "After what we've been through today, it would fit right in."

She shook her head. "I'm sure it was just my imagination. Never mind. I'll see you in the morning."

He stopped her with a hand on her shoulder. "Tell me, Brooke. Please."

She turned slowly back to face him. "When we were climbing out, I thought I saw something behind one of the grates."

The muscles in his stomach tightened. "You saw what, exactly?"

"I thought…" She twisted a strand of hair around her finger. "I thought I saw a pair of eyes watching us." She lifted her chin. "Do you think I imagined it?"

"No, I don't," he said. *But I wish you had.*

Later that evening, Brooke prayed for Victor, for the anguish and confusion she saw deep down in him, the uncertainty that he tried so hard to mask. He was her potential enemy, a man who would be thrilled to convict her father, but she found him to be occupying her thoughts anyway, no matter how chaotic her life had become.

Pulling out her phone, she meant to dial her father until she realized it was nearly eleven, so instead she clicked open the picture of *The Contemplative Lady*. It seemed ridiculous to believe something so beautiful could be hidden away in the ugliness she'd experienced in the tunnels. A delicate painting would never survive, she thought, heart sinking. Her only real hope was that Colda had left some clue down there that would point her to a safer hiding place. She wondered if the police had followed their lead to the missing professor himself. The whole thing might be over by the morning.

Colda could put all the questions to rest. Surely he would corroborate her father's story and Victor and Tuney would have to accept that he was innocent of any wrongdoing. She pulled the covers up to her chin.

Stephanie returned from her shower and climbed into her own bed. "What a day," she said with a sigh.

"Unbelievable," Brooke agreed. "What do you think the next step should be?"

Stephanie chuckled. "Are you afraid I'll say 'Go home and forget the whole thing'?"

"Actually, yes."

"No chance of that," Stephanie said with a yawn. "My brother needs to finish this. Victor is on a mission. I've never seen him so engaged, not since Jennifer died."

"He thinks he'll find a lead back to the museum theft, to Jennifer's killer."

"That's part of it, but I think there's something more motivating him than a painting. We've found treasures before, and this is something different."

Different? Brooke didn't know what to say. Her stomach did a strange flip. What could be motivating Victor to plow through filthy tunnels except the chance to find a Tarkenton or put Jennifer's death to rest? "Did you know Jennifer well?"

"Very. She was a complete scatterbrain, an outgoing, extroverted woman who made Victor a different man." She rolled over onto her stomach. "I hope he can find his way back to that man, someday. Good night, Brooke."

"Good night," she said, trying to picture Victor Gage as he had been before the day both their lives had fallen apart. With thoughts of his green-gold eyes lingering in her mind, she drifted off to sleep.

Brooke woke abruptly. The darkness left her momentarily disoriented. She was cold, the thin blanket insufficient to block the chilly San Francisco air. Stephanie lay quietly in her bed, her breath slow and regular.

Brooke could barely make out the time on her watch, three-fifteen. What had awakened her? The lumpy mattress or the cold? The lingering memories of nearly being crushed in the collapsing tunnel? She closed her eyes and tried to relax until a noise slithered through the room.

She sat up, heart pounding.

Quiet filled up the spaces again; nothing moving, nothing at all.

It must have been a dream.

The room settled into a silence so profound she could hear the tiny ticking from her watch.

A faint scraping noise sounded again and her pulse leaped in her throat. What was it? Something under the bed?

No.

It was farther away, a mournful scrape interrupted by a clank of metal. Then silence.

Downstairs?

Their dorm room was on the bottom floor so the only thing below them was the basement.

She shook her head and listened again.

Nothing but quiet and the relentless ticking of her watch. She considered waking Stephanie, but a seed of doubt bubbled to the surface. She might have imagined it. The details rolled into her mind before she could screen them out, the medical textbook entry she'd practically memorized.

A hallmark of FXTAS symptoms is cognitive or intellectual decline including short-term memory loss, loss of math or spelling skills, difficulty making decisions, personality or mood changes and loss of other intellectual skills.

It sounded so clinical, so benign on paper, until she began to watch the devastating effects play out in front of her eyes. Maybe Tad's affliction was easier. His version of the Fragile X disorder left him impaired from birth, but he'd been even-tempered and genial until he hit his twenties. Her father's mutation of the gene let him live a normal life, free to pursue his passionate interest in art, but now she saw him turning into someone else, an old man who sometimes could not remember who she was, who became angry and irrational without provocation.

Her eyes burned and she pressed her cold fingers to them. *I'm not crazy. Just tired.* The trembling in her body was not the horrible parkinsonism that was part and parcel of her family disease.

Deep breath. Just a nightmare. Go back to sleep.

Forcing her head back onto the pillow, she prayed silently for strength to overcome the fear she still felt eddying inside her like the gray fog outside.

Sleep, Brooke. It will be fine in the morning.

Three minutes later when she heard the noise again, she could contain her terror no longer.

"Stephanie," she whispered, shaking her by the shoulder.

Stephanie jerked awake, eyes wide. "What is it?"

"I heard something. Listen."

The seconds ticked by into minutes.

Brooke met Stephanie's questioning look. "I...I heard something scraping below us."

"In the basement?"

They listened for another long moment. Brooke felt her cheeks warm in spite of the cold. "I don't hear it anymore. I shouldn't have woken you up."

But Stephanie didn't reply. She was up and throwing on jeans and a sweatshirt.

"Where are you going?" Brooke called softly.

"To the basement to check it out," Stephanie said.

Brooke gaped. "You can't do that. It isn't safe."

She smiled. "I'm pretty good at taking care of things, just ask my brothers. And no, I'm not going to go over there and wake Victor up only to find out it's a rat or something, so don't even suggest it."

After a moment of hesitation, Brooke pulled on her

own clothes. "I think your brother would say this is a bad idea, but I'm going with you."

"You're right," Stephanie said cheerfully. "That's exactly what he would say, among other less polite things."

It did not make Brooke feel any better as she followed Stephanie into the darkened hallway.

They walked softly, their feet barely making a sound on the tile as they moved toward the stairwell, flashlight beams zigzagging.

This is crazy, Brooke wanted to shout. *We should not be wandering around darkened buildings at three in the morning.* But there was no way she was going to let Stephanie face any potential danger on her own.

They entered the stairwell, which seemed to be several degrees colder. Brooke held her teeth together to keep them from chattering. No strange noises greeted them in the stairwell except the hollow echo of their own steps. Stephanie paused at the entrance to the basement.

"Ready?"

"No," Brooke whispered.

"Would you feel better if I told you I used to wrestle with my brothers all the time?" Stephanie didn't wait for an answer. She pushed open the door and beamed her flashlight around the basement. When nothing unusual appeared she snapped on the light.

It was just as they had left it. Empty and cold.

Brooke felt her stomach tie itself into knots. She'd

been wrong, hearing things that weren't there. "I'm so sorry, Stephanie."

"No problem. Things being what they are, it pays to check everything out."

Brooke wondered what Victor would say—probably something courteous like his sister. She shivered, rubbing her hands over her arms. "Let's go back. Maybe we can get a few more hours of sleep."

"Okay," Stephanie said. She turned off the light and held the basement door open for Brooke.

"Thanks," Brooke said, feeling a strange stirring on her neck.

She looked carefully at the metal grates set into the wall.

Was there a flicker?

The telltale sign of a human eye like she thought she'd seen before?

Nothing but the wild stirrings of her imagination.

She stewed over it all the way back to her dorm room. Her mind was conjuring up noises like her father believed he saw people from his youth clustered around him. She should go home. Go back to her father and hide away like she'd done so well until this strange adventure began.

She tried to remember why she'd felt so confident that she would sniff out the Tarkenton in the tunnels of all places. It felt like lunacy now. Was she getting lost now in a fantasy of her own making?

Worse yet, she'd dragged Stephanie and Victor into it, too.

"I'm sorry," she said again to Stephanie. "I'm going crazy, I think." She bit her lip feeling tears crowd her eyes.

"Or maybe you aren't," Stephanie said, pointing to the bed.

There on Brooke's pillow lay a little black pawn.

THIRTEEN

Victor was furious. He sat, jaw clenched, on a chair in the women's dorm room listening to the story unfold.

"So you went down to the basement without coming to get me? In the middle of the night? By yourselves?"

Brooke's face flushed and she looked away, but Stephanie wasn't the least bit chagrined.

"No time for outrage now, brother." She handed him the chess piece wrapped in a plastic bag. "Question is, who left this and why?"

"Maybe it was Colda," Brooke said, hope shining in her face. "He's in hiding in the tunnels."

"Colda is most likely dead," Victor snapped, immediately wishing he hadn't. He was not sure of the source of his anger, but he had the niggling feeling it was born of fear, fear that something might have happened to Stephanie and Brooke.

"Well, who else knows about the pawns?" Stephanie mused.

Victor sighed. He stretched his arms, trying to rid himself of the aches and pains accumulated in the adventure from the previous day. "I'll text Tuney and fill him in, but I'm not sure I trust him completely. Or Lock or Stryker, for that matter. Any of them might have figured out how to get in the dorm and leave it here."

"Are we going down there again?" Brooke said.

He knew she was still hoping, still hanging on to the notion that Colda really had stashed the painting somewhere. Something was definitely going on, but he did not think it was a straightforward game of find-the-treasure anymore. "I'm going with Tuney. You two should stay here and see what you can find out about Colda."

Stephanie shook her head. "Sounds like we're being dismissed."

"I'm not going to let you two keep putting yourself at risk."

"You know I can take care of myself," Stephanie said.

He did, but he didn't feel as sure about Brooke. She was so trusting, so willing to believe people. He watched her now, her face pale, tired shadows darkening her eyes. Why did he feel such a surge of protectiveness? The desperate feeling that if something happened to her he would never be the same? "It's safer. Besides, you might be able to sniff out something about Colda's past that would help, something the cops didn't find and Tuney overlooked."

Stephanie opened her mouth to argue when Brooke's phone rang. As she listened, her face grew even paler. She clicked off the phone and stared at them. "I've got to go to the police station."

"What for?"

"Something they found out about Colda, I think, but they want to speak in person." She gave Victor a shaky look. "They asked for you, also."

Victor felt a quiver deep down. The news wouldn't be good, whatever it was. "All right. Let's go. Steph…"

"I know, I know. Stay out of trouble. I'll go check in at the office. Call me when you have an update."

He nodded and they walked silently to the car. Who had left the pawn? Was it a message or a warning? Brooke was probably wondering the same thing, because they made the drive to the police station in near silence.

After a long, frustrating wait, they were ushered in to see Detective Paulson, a whip-thin man with a fringe of black hair around his balding head. "Thanks for coming. I understand you are exploring the tunnels under the college. How is that going?"

Brooke told him, sending an uneasy glance at Victor when she explained about the pawns painted on the tunnel entrances, and gave him the pawn she'd found on her pillow.

The detective broke into a wide smile. "Comes off like a bad movie. College kids probably painted all kinds of things down there. At least once a week we're in those tunnels trying to coax them out after they busted through a grate or something. Nothing down there but pipes, we tell them, but it's the mystique that pulls them in."

Victor knew it was more than mystique that pulled Colda into those tunnels, but he didn't share his thoughts. "Have you found him? Professor Colda?"

The detective's face grew sober. "Possibly."

"What does that mean?"

"It means we found his car."

Brooke sat bolt upright. "Really? Where?"

"Underwater."

Her eyes rounded in horror. "Is he... Did he drown?"

"Haven't got a body yet. Car was at the bottom of the bay, windows open."

Victor kept his voice low. "Accident?"

The detective slid his glance from Victor to Brooke. "Maybe."

"So why did you call us here, Detective?" Victor said.

"Trouble trail."

"What?"

"I've been at this business since the dawn of time and when someone has this trail of trouble that seems to follow them, it means something is up."

"You sound like Mr. Tuney."

"No doubt. He was a San Francisco cop for years before he got the boot."

Victor could not hide his surprise. "Really? Why was he let go?"

Paulson folded his arms. "His story to tell, not mine. Anyway…" His gaze shifted to Brooke and he took a sip from the orange-juice container on his desk. "You come to town, a woman gets murdered, a woman who was following you. You come to Bayside in search of Professor Colda, a friend of your father's, and now it appears Colda may have killed himself."

Brooke gasped, hands clenched. "Oh, no. That's horrible."

"He mailed us a letter that we received today. Reads as follows." The detective consulted a photocopy. "'I can't take the guilt anymore from what I did four years ago. I ruined a good man who had nothing to do with the museum robbery. I'm sorry, Donald. I hope this will clear your name, friend. L. Colda.'"

She felt tears crowd her eyes. "You see? He didn't do it. My father is innocent, just like I said. He had nothing to do with the theft or Jennifer's death." She looked at Victor with utter joy suffusing her face.

How he wished it was true, but a glance at Paulson told him the other shoe hadn't yet dropped.

"We're not quite there yet," Paulson said. "As a matter of fact, a couple of things make us question the suicide theory and here's one of them." He flipped an eight-by-ten glossy photo on the desk so Victor and Brooke could examine it.

Brooke gasped and sat up, electrified. "It's a pencil sketch. One of the works that was stolen from the museum."

Victor leaned forward, peering at the photo of a small framed picture. He'd never actually seen photos of the stolen items. "This was in Colda's car?"

"Nope."

"Where, then?" Brooke said, a wary tone creeping into her voice.

"In a box stored at the group home where your brother, Tad, stays."

Brooke's face drained of color. "No. No, that's not possible. My brother has Fragile X Syndrome. Surely you don't think…"

Paulson waved a hand. "Of course not, but someone stored the thing there and it wasn't Colda. According to both Donald and Denise, he hadn't met Tad, and the group home confirms he'd never even visited there."

"Oh, no. You think my father was hiding it there? For what reason would he do that?"

Paulson stared at her without a hint of a smile. "He probably sold the other two and waited to find a buyer for this one. He stashed it there, or had someone else do it."

"Me?" Brooke said, her voice an anguished cry.

"Or Denise. Or maybe even Jeffrey Lock—he visited Tad one time and brought some artwork for the inmates, so to speak."

"My brother is not an inmate," she hissed.

"My apologies. Slip of the tongue."

Victor felt the wall of bitterness wash over him, as he pictured Donald using his disabled son to hide the stolen goods. Brooke's father engineered the robbery that killed Jennifer. He was responsible, as surely as if he'd driven the car that smashed into theirs.

"You're wrong," Brooke mumbled, as if speaking to him. "It wasn't me or my father, or my aunt. I don't know how the sketch got there unless Dean Lock put it there himself."

"And we'll talk to him about that, you can believe it." Detective Paulson gave her a look that was not without pity. "I'm sorry, Ms. Ramsey. I know this is hard to hear. I wanted to apprise you of the situation and let you know that we're reopening the investigation into the theft four years ago."

She let out a choked sob. "But my father is…he's mentally failing. You can't interrogate him, please."

Paulson held up a calming hand. "We've spoken to his doctor and confirmed that. We'll continue to check into the details as best we can. We've already contacted Denise Ramsey and she's been very cooperative. We'll reinterview Dean Lock, the security guards and any of Colda's contacts that we can find, though he wasn't much of a social butterfly." He shuffled some papers on his desk. "We will get to the truth, with or without your father's help."

Victor fixed the detective with a stare. "What do you think happened to Colda?"

"My theory?"

Victor nodded.

Paulson drained the orange juice and slam-dunked the container into the trash can. "I think someone killed him, faked the suicide note and made it look like he drove himself into the bay."

"Can you prove it?"

"As I said. Just a theory at this point."

"But what about the Tarkenton my father sent to Bayside?" Brooke said, her voice desperate.

Paulson's eyes were cold. "As far as that goes, there's no proof that such a painting ever existed. Only painting we've got here is the one in Colda's apartment."

"I saw the original, my father saw it, Aunt Denise saw it. We all did."

"Three people who all have reason to want Donald's name cleared. You could have made the whole story up."

"But why would we do that? What purpose would it serve?"

He leaned back in his chair. "I don't know, Ms. Ramsey. Maybe you could tell me."

Brooke didn't utter a sound.

Paulson showed them out to the waiting area and left.

Victor did not trust himself to speak. They stood there in an unexpectedly sunny afternoon, but he felt no joy in it. Her father was behind the plot that killed Jennifer. And here he was, wrapped up in an investigation because he thought he could ferret ou what happened four years before. The situation had grown more complicated. The painful truth was, he felt something for Brooke, some strange attraction that pulled him into her orbit.

The guilt welled up inside. He'd helped her, assisting her to find yet another treasure for her father.

Brooke finally spoke. "It isn't true." Her eyes searched his and he knew she was desperate to see some kindness there, a flicker of trust.

"That's not how it looks," was the gentlest thing he could say.

"You know I didn't hide that sketch at Tad's group home. I would never..." A sob choked off her words. "I would never use my brother."

His throat felt a little thick, too. "I know you wouldn't, and I know you didn't have anything to do with what your father did."

She pressed her lips together and blinked back the tears. "He didn't do it. You need to believe me. I know the truth."

"You can't see the truth," he said, jaw tight. "You love your father too much."

"Just as much as you loved your wife," she said, turning and walking back to the car.

She willed herself not to cry. The nightmare was taking over her life again after so many years of grief. It could not be happening.

Father, help me, she prayed silently.

The wall that had sprung up between her and

Victor was acutely painful, though she was not sure why. He'd never believed her father's innocence. It should be no surprise that he greeted her with only cold suspicion now.

She would go home. Book the next flight out. Pay Victor whatever his time was worth and rush to her father's side.

As soon as Victor parked the car, Brooke hurried to the courtyard, a quiet spot where she could make a call back home. No answer. Frustration almost overcame her. She felt like hurling the phone onto the paving stones just to see it smash.

Do not give in to despair, she told herself.

Chin up.

She walked into the dorm room to pack her things. She found Victor and Stephanie deep in discussion. They broke off when she entered. "I'm going back to San Diego. I'll pay you for your time," she said stiffly.

Victor didn't move, just stared at her, his face an unreadable mask.

A knock on the door startled them all and Brooke's mouth fell open as Denise walked in. She could not say a word, only threw herself into her aunt's arms and cried. Denise squeezed her back and whispered something comforting that Brooke could not make out. Finally she pulled away.

"Dad. Is he okay?"

Denise squeezed Brooke's hand, her grip strong in spite of her sixty-two years. "Perfectly fine. I've hired a nurse to care for him until I get back—Mrs. Jones, you know her—and an attorney to make sure he doesn't incriminate himself in any way. He's not lucid right now, so the police have agreed to give us a little time." She tucked her auburn bob behind her ear and turned to the Gages. "Your secretary told me I would find you here, Mr. Gage."

Brooke wiped her eyes. "You should stay with Dad. They're reopening the case."

She pursed her lips for a moment. "I've been told all about that and that's why I'm here. You and I both know your father didn't steal anything, nor did he have anything to do with Colda's disappearance or suicide or whatever it was. Your dad sent that painting here and if there's the smallest chance we can find it, and prove that he wasn't working with Colda now or back then when the museum sketches were snatched, then I'm here to help you do that."

Brooke hugged her again, profoundly relieved to have someone in her corner, someone who knew the truth about her father. Denise gave her a pat and turned to the others. "You've heard the whole story from the police?"

Victor nodded and introduced his sister. He brushed a hand through his hair. "Ms. Ramsey, I think you should know that there is a minuscule chance that there is anything of value in those tunnels. They're dangerous and filthy and…"

She cut him off. "And you think Donald has

already stolen the painting from Colda and killed him, made it look like a suicide."

The abrupt remark made Victor blink. "Possibly," he said simply.

Denise smiled. "I can see where you might think that, but I have the advantage of knowing you are wrong about Donald, so there's every chance you're wrong about the tunnels. I came to help. A few days, and if we find nothing, then Brooke and I fly home. I know the theft all those years ago cost you your wife and I'm very sorry about that. I understand why you don't want to help any longer, Mr. Gage. Thank you for keeping Brooke safe."

Victor's jaw tightened and Brooke could see the hardness in his face. "I didn't take this case just to find your painting. I took it because I thought there might be a connection to what happened four years ago."

"And it seems there is, but the guilt is on Colda's shoulders now," Denise said calmly.

"And Donald's."

Denise shook her head, a hint of impatience creeping in. "Colda confessed in his letter and if anyone was working with Colda on the museum theft, it wasn't Donald."

"Then who was it?" Victor asked, voice low.

Denise shook her head. "The only other person it could be."

Victor raised an eyebrow. "Dean Lock?"

Her lips thinned. "I know him better than any of

you." She sucked in a breath. "Things being how they are, I understand that you won't want to work with us anymore on this."

Victor stood still for a moment, then nodded slowly. "We'll leave you two alone now."

Brooke watched through the window as Victor left, the urge to run to him rippling through her body. In a moment, he would be gone, out of her life permanently, swallowed up into the world and she would never see him again.

Victor, don't go. You're wrong about my father, wrong about everything.

But she didn't say a word as he walked out of the dorm and out of her life.

Aunt Denise put a hand on her shoulder. "He's a handsome man."

"Yes," she said faintly.

"Let's start making some plans, Brooke."

Pushing down the strange tearing sensation in her chest, she turned and followed her aunt to the table.

FOURTEEN

Victor packed mechanically, precisely, the way he did everything else in his life. The police would handle things now, ferret out the connection between Colda and Donald. They'd make the case and convict him, if he was fit enough to stand trial.

So why didn't Victor feel the surge of satisfaction he'd been coveting for four years? He was a treasure seeker who had found no treasure, that must be it. Professional disappointment, a waste of time and resources for the agency.

Stephanie flopped on the bed, staring at him. "So we're walking away?"

"Why wouldn't we? There's no treasure here. I got what I came for."

"You don't look very happy about it."

He added his flashlight to the pack. "I was after more than the Tarkenton."

"I know," she said softly. "And the police finding those stolen sketches at the group home pins it neatly on Brooke's father. You got what you came for."

"Donald may have been the mastermind, but he wasn't the driver who crashed into us. And none of this brings Jennifer back."

"No, it doesn't." Stephanie rolled onto her back and put her hands behind her head. "And we don't even have the pleasure of finding a treasure for our trouble." She paused. "There's also the matter of the pawn."

"The one left on Brooke's bed?"

"Yep. If Colda's the bad guy and he's floating in the bay after killing himself, then who put it there?"

Victor didn't admit it, but the same question had been prodding at him, also. "Stryker?"

"For what purpose?"

"A joke?"

She shook her head. "I don't see him as the joking type. He's after something."

Victor zipped his bag closed. "Doesn't matter. The bigger issue is that Donald Ramsey arranged the museum theft and now Colda's dead so we may never know where the painting is, or even if it ever was here in the first place."

She sat up. "But something is going on here, something that may impact Brooke."

His gut squeezed. "She has her aunt to help her now."

"That might not be enough."

He didn't answer. "We came for treasure. That's our job. There's no treasure so it's time to pull the plug."

"Quit seeing everything in black or white. You

know that whatever Brooke's father did or didn't do, it had nothing to do with her."

"Yes, it does."

Her eyes widened. "No more than you are connected to our dad's decisions. Or responsible for the bad choices I made. Brooke is not a part of what happened to Jennifer. You can't paint her with that brush."

Blood pounded in his veins. "I don't want to be tangled up in her life."

"That's okay as long as you're clear about the reasons. Is it because she's Donald's daughter? Or you're scared because you're attracted to her?"

He spun on his heel to face his sister. "I'm not attracted to her."

"That so? Then why do you smile when she's around? You laugh, think about things other than balancing the books or reading dusty references about Vermeers and Treskilling stamps."

His face grew hot. "There's no one for me. Jennifer was it, Steph, so don't try to fix me up, especially with Brooke Ramsey."

She shrugged. "Just calling it like I see it, brother, even though you refuse to."

"Enough, Stephanie." He clamped his jaws together to keep from snapping at her. *I've got no feelings for any woman and I never will.*

Tuney rapped a knuckle on the open door. "Got a minute?"

"Yes," Victor said, gesturing him to a chair. "We're pulling out of Bayside."

"I got your text message and the photo of the pawn. Now you figure the whole treasure in the tunnel thing is a wild-goose hunt, huh? I could have told you that. Oh, wait. I did tell you that."

Victor ignored the sarcasm. "I'll call the dean and clue him in."

Tuney folded his arms. "Couple things before you go. Checked in with the cops. They didn't find Colda's body yet."

"Is that unusual?" Stephanie asked, pulling up a chair. "Could be it was washed away?"

"Could be."

Victor eyed him. "Are you thinking Colda didn't die in that car?"

Tuney didn't appear to hear the question. He let the words trickle out slowly, like the first drops of rain before a storm. "Let me tell you the other thing. The chess piece, the pawn, it's Colda's."

Victor straightened.

"What?" Stephanie said. "How did you figure that?"

"When the professor first disappeared, I poked around, talked to a lot of students. The guy was a big chess enthusiast, used to challenge the students to matches and generally he won. Here's the thing. He always brought his own chess set, an antique from 1850, boxwood and ebony. He called it his lady friend. Kind of pathetic, really. Guy really was an oddball."

"And the pawn on Brooke's bed?" Stephanie said. "Was it from that set?"

He nodded. "Black ebony with the green registration sticker on the bottom."

Victor fought his way through the surprise. "So Colda put this on Stephanie's pillow? He's alive?"

"Or someone who has Colda's chess set."

"How could Colda or anyone else have gotten into the dorm that night? I checked all the exit doors and windows. All locked from the inside." Victor closed his eyes and sighed. "Of course. He came in through the basement passage or some other that we don't know about."

"Guy's a regular phantom," Tuney agreed. "Who knew an old dried-up professor could get around so well?"

Victor's nerves prickled. If Colda was alive and in hiding on the campus, then he would do anything to discourage people from flushing him out. People like Brooke and her aunt.

Tuney's eyes glittered. "So you'll be staying, then? Keeping an eye out until the search is officially over?"

"Why does it matter to you? The university will be happy to get rid of us, seems to me," Victor observed.

He stood. "Just doing my job."

Victor looked closely at Tuney. "Your investigations have been very thorough. I'm surprised the university would go to such lengths to find their professor. Why not let the cops handle it?"

"Not my concern as long as they're paying me."

"You're good at finding things out."

"Used to be a pretty effective cop back in the day."

"Paulson mentioned you'd worked for SFPD."

Tuney grimaced. "Then I guess he told you I got canned. I didn't say I was a good cop, just effective. Anyway, I've got a personal motive. Fran is dead, though everyone seems to have forgotten that fact, and I'm staying on this like stink on cheese until someone pays."

Victor hadn't forgotten. He also knew that the need for revenge fed on itself until it consumed a person. Tuney wasn't about to be put off the trail anytime soon. "Question. Back during your investigations after the museum theft, did you know that Dean Lock and Donald Ramsey were friends?"

"Yeah."

"Close enough that Lock visited Donald's son, Tad?"

Tuney cocked his head. "I didn't know that. What are you getting at?"

Victor shrugged, not really sure himself. "Struck me as odd, is all."

"The whole thing is odd, so keep me apprised about the next foray down below," Tuney said.

"I told you we're leaving," Victor said.

Tuney grinned. "You're not leaving."

"And how do you know that?" Victor said.

"Because if there's a chance Colda's alive, then there's still a chance you can put your hands on that Tarkenton. You're not going to walk away from that."

"You're wrong," Victor said.

Tuney left him with an ironic smile. Victor stared after him, thoughts dancing around his mind. Brooke. Colda. Donald. A priceless painting that might lie just yards below his feet.

Stephanie was already on her laptop before Tuney cleared the building.

"Checking on something," she said. A moment later, she reached for her cell phone.

Victor circled the room, energy surging through him, the same energy that had filled him before they found the Vermeer and the dozen treasures before that. They were close, he was sure. But something hummed through his thoughts that had nothing to do with treasure.

Was Colda alive or dead? Had he left the pawn, and what message was he sending? What they'd mistaken for eccentricity might be flat-out insanity, and insanity could be a very dangerous thing.

Stephanie interrupted his thoughts.

"Left a message for the university president."

Victor raised an eyebrow. "You went right to the top of the food chain. Do you think he'll return your call?"

"I left Dad's name. He'll call."

"What are you checking on, exactly?"

"It suddenly struck me that maybe Tuney isn't really employed by the university after all."

"What would be his motive for lying?"

She held up open palms. "At this point, who could guess?"

Victor nodded. "The whole situation gets murkier by the moment. Is anyone telling the truth in this whole mess?"

Brooke. The name materialized in his mind. Donald was a criminal, but she knew him only as a loving father. That meant she had an enormous blind spot, a blind spot that just might get her killed.

"Finished packing?" Stephanie said innocently.

"Thinking," he growled.

Stephanie smiled.

By late afternoon, Brooke and Denise had made their plans. The following morning, Brooke would try to retrace the path she'd taken the day before, hoping to find a route around the collapsed section. Stephanie had given her the map already, and she and Denise pored over it, cobbling together a route to explore.

As they plotted, Brooke told her aunt about the pawn left on her pillow the night before.

Denise's gray eyes widened in shock. "Here? In this room? Who left it there? Not Colda."

Brooke shook her head. "I just don't know. It doesn't seem to make any sense at all." She sat back, uneasily. "Another thing is, there's the possibility that we won't be allowed to stay to figure any of this out."

"Lock?"

She nodded. "Victor strong-armed him into co-operating, and since he isn't going to work with us anymore, Lock may just throw us out on our ear."

Denise took her hand and Brooke was comforted by the look of strength on her face. "We'll face it one step at a time, honey, like we've done with everything else."

Brooke felt close to tears again. "I just want everything to be okay, for Dad to have his moment and Tad to come home."

She gave Brooke a final pat. "We'll keep pushing forward. That's all we can do."

They didn't have to wait long to find out the dean's thoughts on the subject. He hobbled up using one crutch for support as they exited the dorm. He looked closer at Denise, who stood a head shorter than Brooke.

"What are you doing here?"

"Nice to see you again, too, Jeffrey."

Brooke looked from the dean to her aunt.

Denise turned to Brooke. "The dean and I go way back. We were college sweethearts, weren't we?"

An edge in her tone told Brooke the relationship didn't bring back fond memories for her aunt.

"That was a long time ago," the dean said, cheeks pink in his pale face. "I thought that was old history."

"It is, on my part," Denise said, "but I didn't think

you could leave it all in the past. That's why I didn't offer to come with you in the first place, Brooke. I thought the dean would be more cooperative if I wasn't there to stir up bad memories."

The dean exhaled loudly. "This situation has nothing to do with what passed between us in the past, Denise." He focused on Brooke. "Victor tells me they're finished and going home."

Brooke swallowed hard. She'd known it, but hearing about his departure caused a fresh pain inside her heart.

It's better for him to go, Brooke. You're getting your feelings all confused. Distance would be the best thing.

"You need to do the same," Lock continued. "For your own safety."

"That's very kind of you to think about our wellbeing," Denise said. "I wish you had been more inclined to think about our family when you blamed Donald for the museum theft."

Lock's lips thinned. "There were two people with the delivery schedule," he hissed. "Donald and myself. I know I wasn't behind the heist."

"I don't," Denise said flatly. "I know exactly what kind of man you are, you showed that to me forty years ago. Donald didn't rob his own museum."

"You're implying I did."

"Not implying," she said. "Colda mailed a note to the police claiming he was responsible, but he must have gotten the delivery schedule from someone."

Brooke's stomach knotted. This was a man they had to placate, and her aunt was succeeding only in throwing gasoline on the fire.

"Can we leave that for the moment?" she said, holding up a calming hand. "We're here just to find my father's Tarkenton. We need to explore the tunnel again and examine Colda's apartment one more time."

"Without your Treasure Seekers?" the dean said.

Brooke nodded. "Yes."

"Too dangerous. The university would never allow it."

Denise cocked her head. "You can allow it. You did before. You can do it again."

"I could," he said, leveling a look full of hate at Denise. "But I won't."

"Please, Dean Lock," Brooke said, stepping forward. "We have reason to believe Colda faked his suicide, that he's still alive and in the tunnels."

Lock's eyes widened. "And you still believe Colda may have hidden the painting down there? This Tarkenton your father pretends to have found?"

Denise tensed but Brooke laid a hand on her arm. "Yes."

"That's idiocy. I've said so from the start, but I indulged you because Mr. Gage is a benefactor of this university. You've found absolutely zero evidence so far, only a bad picture painted by Colda, something he dreamed up on his own."

"It will cost you nothing for us to take a look, and

if I'm right, think of the reward, an unknown Tarkenton revealed to the world, found at your university."

His eyes glistened with the same desire, the near fanaticism that her own father displayed when he spoke about a master painting. For a moment, Brooke felt sick, but she thought that very zeal might just cause him to acquiesce.

She was wrong.

"No," he said curtly. "You're welcome to check out his apartment again but that's it. Pack up your things and be out by sunrise tomorrow. You're not authorized to be on this campus anymore."

FIFTEEN

Brooke felt numb. All the effort, the worry had come down to a big, fat dead end.

Denise's expression was anguished. "I'm so sorry, honey. I should have kept my mouth shut, but when I saw him there, it all came out."

"It's okay," Brooke said, forcing an optimistic tone. "At least we can look at Colda's place one more time. Maybe we'll see something we missed before." She puzzled over the earlier text she'd received from Victor.

Pawn belonged to Colda.

Be careful.

Careful. Why would he care about that? Pain surged inside. She shook away images of him as they walked across the nearly dark campus. Brooke tried to think of how to bring up the subject of Denise's contentious past with Lock. Her aunt spared her the trouble.

"I loved him once. Jeffrey, I mean. We were college freshmen together and he was a budding pianist.

Brilliant, too. I loved his passion for music and art. He seemed so much more alive than anyone else I'd ever met." She smiled sadly. "I made some bad decisions and got pregnant."

Brooke tried not to show her surprise. "I didn't know."

"No one did. I was young and foolish, stubborn, too. A baby was not something Jeffrey pictured in his life. It would strip away his freedom to pursue his ambition. He wanted me to end the pregnancy, but I couldn't. Instead I dropped out of school, used my college money for the doctor bills and the delivery." She blinked hard. "The baby was stillborn. I called Jeffrey and told him about it. He said he was sorry and not to call him again."

Brooke sighed. "I'm so sorry, Aunt Denise."

She patted Brooke's shoulder. "I don't need your pity, honey. After I buried my daughter, I moved on and so did Jeffrey. I just tell you that so you know what kind of man he is. I knew all along. He should have been found guilty of the museum theft, not your father."

She felt a surge of deep gratitude toward her aunt.

Denise had stepped in and taken up the slack when things in the Ramsey household fell apart after Brooke's mother left. She felt the surge of anger again at her mother who'd skipped out when she was sixteen, unable to handle a moody husband and a disturbed son.

Your loss, Mom. We're a good little family, and I'm going to make sure we stay that way.

The urgency to solve the riddle rose ever stronger inside her. She had to get home to her father and Tad, to take responsibility for them again and make everything okay. If she could just find something, any tiny clue that would hint at where Colda had hidden the painting and possibly explain how the stolen sketch wound up with Tad.

They let themselves in using the key Lock provided them.

Denise whistled at the mess. "And I thought your father was untidy." She examined the reproduction of the Tarkenton closely as Brooke pointed out the misplaced pawns.

"Incredible. I never would have figured that out."

"I had help." Her heart squeezed at the thought of Victor. He was undoubtedly gone, ensconced in his office perhaps, researching for the next treasure to find.

She flashed on his face in the tunnel when he could not escape, vulnerable, desperate.

Lord, help him find his way to You, she prayed in spite of the pain that knifed through her.

Denise was riffling through the file cabinets. "Colda must have left some notes, something about the Tarkenton."

Brooke left her to her digging and went to the small bedroom. The drawers had already been searched, even under the mattress. Heavy drapes covered the windows but she felt the whisper of cool air, evidence of an open window. She pulled them aside, gazing down into the darkness below.

She saw a flicker on the glass.

It was not coming from outside, but rather it was a reflection of movement behind her.

With a scream she started to whirl around as a figure shoved past her, an arm knocking her to the floor. The window was yanked open further and in a moment the man was gone, shimmying down the gutter pipe.

"Stop," Brooke yelled, scrambling to her feet. She ran back out of the bedroom, nearly plowing into her aunt, who was in the process of running to help her. "A man," she gasped as she careened by, through the hall and down the front steps.

She stopped there, panting, listening.

A scuffling in the bushes to her left made her take off running again.

Suddenly someone stepped in front of her and she crashed into a set of sturdy shoulders, bringing them both to the ground. She rolled over and found herself nose to nose with a prostrate Victor. She struggled to her knees and he did the same, helping her to her feet in time to see Stephanie trotting out from the tree line.

"Gone," she said. "Back into the tunnel, the cover wasn't quite pulled closed."

Victor brushed the grass from his shirtfront. "Steph and I were walking and we heard a scream. Was that you?"

She nodded, trying to catch her breath.

Denise ran up. "I messaged the police. There was a man in Colda's place. What did he look like?"

Brooke tried to collect her thoughts. "I don't know. It was dark and he was moving fast."

"Stryker? Colda?" Victor demanded.

"Tuney?" Stephanie put in.

Brooke sighed. "I'm not sure. It happened too fast. I think he was hiding under the bed when I came in. I didn't get a good look."

"What would someone want in the professor's house?" Stephanie said. "Nothing there worth anything."

"Except maybe to the professor," Victor said.

"Actually, I think there might be something of interest," Denise said slowly. "Come with me."

The silence was broken only by the chirping of a cricket somewhere in the grass as they filed back into the professor's apartment. She still felt Victor's arms encircling her after she fell, strong and warm.

Denise gestured them to the table and pulled out a torn piece of paper. "It was in one of the files."

Brooke saw only some nearly illegible scribbles. "Can you tell what that says?"

"Only because I've been hanging around with

your father for too long," she said. "'No gr. shine. Fx indic.'"

"Does that mean something to you?" Stephanie asked.

"Let me expand on it and see if you recognize any of the terms. I think he's saying, 'No graphite shine, foxing indicated.' Ring any bells?"

Victor nodded slowly. "I heard chapter and verse on this when we were searching for the Vermeer." Excitement shone in his eyes. "*Graphite shine* refers to the pencil work. If the shine hasn't oxidized then the work is modern and potentially a fake. *Foxing* is the brown mildew spots that occur on older work."

"So these are authentication notes," Stephanie said.

"The Tarkenton," Brooke breathed, her skin prickling.

"Maybe," Victor said. "But it doesn't indicate that painting specifically."

Denise put a small object on the table, no bigger than a paper clip. "This was taped to the back. It's an unusual wood, silvery in color with green undertones. I've seen it before."

Brooke watched a slow smile form on her aunt's face. "I have, too. It's a piece of the Tarkenton frame, isn't it?"

"I think so," Denise said. "He no doubt removed a piece to send it out for infrared spectroscopy."

"To prove the age of the painting," Victor said.

Stephanie laughed. "Pretty high-tech. How did we miss that in our search?"

"You might have seen it and not even realized what it was," Denise said.

Victor grunted. "I don't like missing things."

Denise ignored the comment. She looked away, eyes darting back and forth in thought. "Colda would have started out by doing a provenance analysis, like Donald and I did. Is the piece recorded in reference books? Researching the original owners, searching for letters of authentication. Donald found only a few oblique references to the work, and the people running the estate sale where he bought it had no idea how it even got there. There were only a few vague hints in some archived letters from Tarkenton that the work even existed. Colda would have to go the forensic route. He probably started with a signature analysis."

"We've got some proof now." Brooke couldn't contain her excitement. She sprang from the table. "It really is a Tarkenton. Dad is right."

Denise held up a hand. "It leads us in that direction, but this is still not concrete."

Brooke walked to the reproduction of *The Contemplative Lady*. "If he knew or strongly suspected it was the real thing, he should have let my father know."

"Unless he intended to take it for himself. Sell it, maybe."

Victor frowned. "It would be incredibly hard

to sell a painting like that. You'd have to go black market, and find a collector."

"Which would take some time," Stephanie added.

Brooke's eyes roved the familiar picture. "So you'd need to find a good hiding place in the meanwhile."

Denise nodded. "Someplace no one would ever think to look."

Soon they were all four gazing at the picture, the little black pawns advancing across the chessboard. "Maybe even fake your own death," Victor murmured.

Brooke looked at Victor, who stared steadfastly at the painting. "The dean asked us to leave by morning. He and my aunt are not on good terms."

Stephanie cocked her head and gave her brother a sidelong glance. "The investigation is over for us, too."

"But now with this," Denise said, "you could get Jeffrey to rethink things."

Victor continued to stare but Brooke saw a glimmer in his eye. "In light of this new information, I think our plans have changed."

The dean's face was suffused with anger, the lines harsh on his face in the office light. They had caught him on his way out, surprised to find him still working at nearly seven o'clock. It was just Victor and Brooke, and Victor had the overwhelming feeling of déjà vu as he sat there. Brooke was trying to go for calm, but he could feel the energy radiating off her.

She'd never win a poker game, he thought, hiding a smile. It wouldn't change things even if they did find the Tarkenton, now that her father was concretely linked to the museum robbery, but for whatever reason, he was glad, at that moment, to be sitting there next to her.

"There's been a modification in the schedule," the dean growled. "The demolition starts Monday."

Victor raised an eyebrow. "That's fast. What caused the change?"

Lock waved a hand. "Who knows? I'm not in charge of construction details."

Victor glanced around the office, pristine from the polished wood desk to the upright antique piano. "But you aren't packing up?"

"Our offices were renovated last year, they won't be touched."

"Fine, then. We'll be out by Sunday night. That gives us two more days."

"To find the Tarkenton? By then they may have found Colda. Or his body." The dean, Victor noticed, did not appear overly concerned about the prospect.

Brooke tensed. Was she still holding out hope that Colda could be found and somehow explain how he'd hidden the sketch at Tad's himself, absolving her father of guilt? Not likely. Not remotely likely. "Dean Lock, there's the chance that Colda is hiding in the tunnels."

Lock started visibly. "Ms. Ramsey implied something like that, but it's preposterous."

Victor relayed the details of the intruder at the Professor House and the pawn found on Brooke's pillow.

Lock's eyes popped. "This is insane, some sort of crazy story you're cooking up to continue this ridiculous farce. There's no treasure, and Colda is dead or long gone. The only good to come of it is that now the truth is out. He cooked up the museum robbery with Donald. I had nothing to do with it, not that I will ever get another shot at a curatorship again." His face creased into a bitter mask. "Once there's a whiff of impropriety, no matter how undeserved, that's the end."

"You don't have to tell me that." Brooke's voice was sad. "If Colda is dead then my father might never get a chance to clear his name either."

Victor stepped in before Lock could give voice to the anger kindling in his eyes.

"We'll be out by Sunday night."

"If you aren't, I'm calling the police."

Victor held the door for Brooke on the way out. He spotted a small wooden chessboard on display, all the pieces lined up in perfect order. No pawns missing, he noticed idly. He gestured to the board. "Do you play, Dean Lock?"

Lock paused for a moment. "Yes."

"Did you ever play with Colda?"

"Occasionally."

"With his chess set?"

He nodded. "We stopped a few months ago."

"Why?"

"Because I have more important things to do and Colda was annoying and feebleminded."

Victor saw the truth behind the words.

And because you hate to lose.

He joined Brooke and they headed outside where they met an arriving police officer. It was another hour before they finished and Victor walked Brooke back to the dorm.

He felt suddenly awkward, unsure about what to say to her. *Stick to business, Victor.*

"We'll go in tomorrow at sunrise. I'll text Tuney."

She didn't answer. As they walked into a patch of moonlight, she turned her face to his. "Thank you. I know you're only doing this because there's the possibility of finding a Tarkenton, but I want you to know I appreciate it."

The moonlight gilded her hair and lit the smooth contours of her face, her full lips and delicate brows. The urge rose inside him, strong and unexpected, the desire to pull her to him and press those lips to his.

She's right, he told himself. *You're here for the treasure and for the truth.*

But the feeling in his gut would not go away as he walked her to her dorm, a strange mixture of worry and longing, a desperate need to hold on to Brooke Ramsay.

He wondered if it would disappear when and if he held *The Contemplative Lady* in his hands.

SIXTEEN

Brooke found Stephanie and Denise whispering when she woke before sunup.

"Sorry, honey. Thought we'd let you sleep a few more minutes. You tossed and turned last night."

Brooke sighed. Dreams had kept her sleep fitful at best, dreams of her father and Tad. She held them both by the hand, pulling them along in desperate flight through long and twisting corridors. She woke in a sweat-soaked panic, only to fall asleep again, this time to odd flickers of Victor climbing a rusted ladder and growing ever farther away.

Victor is here to find the Tarkenton and destroy your father, she chastised herself. *He's not your friend.*

Nonetheless, as she closed her eyes and whispered her prayers, she found Victor again front and center in her thoughts.

"We found some info on Stryker," Stephanie said. "His name really is Stryker, last name Leeds. He's been a taxi driver in California for a while."

Brooke heard in Stephanie's tone that there was something else. "Where in California?"

"San Francisco."

Her heart thumped. "This is getting to be like a bad movie."

"He drove the neighborhood of your father's museum."

Brooke shook her head. "And now he just happens to show up here?"

"Curiouser and curiouser, to quote Alice," Denise said with a frown. "But we'd better focus on the day ahead. I have a feeling it's going to require all our powers of concentration."

Stephanie checked her watch. "Hate to miss out on this adventure, but I need to go pick up my other brother, Luca, at the airport. I've been keeping him apprised of things, and he's about to blow a gasket if he doesn't get in on the action."

"Sounds like Victor," Brooke found herself saying.

"In the determination department they're alike, but Luca's got a silly streak, and he's the kind that lets his heart lead him into trouble."

"And Victor leads with his head, not his heart."

Stephanie finger-combed her short, damp hair. "Yes, but you never know when circumstances will change."

Change? She could not see the intractable Victor being swayed by the stirrings of his heart or soul.

She forced herself to eat a protein bar and packed several more, along with bottled water, into her pack.

Denise did the same and they went to meet Victor at the library.

On the way Stephanie received a message on her phone, which put a smirk on her face. "I knew it."

Brooke had no time to inquire as they entered the silent library, the air stale and scented with the faint aroma of old books.

Tuney was there, scowling as Brooke introduced them.

"We've met," Denise said, declining a handshake. "You've been pestering Donald for four years. Brooke told me you went so far as to hire a woman to follow her."

Tuney's scowl deepened. "And that woman got murdered for her trouble, so there's something going on with the Ramseys, isn't there?"

"No, there isn't, but how about you?" Denise asked. "Were you poking around Colda's place last night?"

"Police already asked me, and no, I've got better things to do with my time," Tuney snapped.

Stephanie stepped in between them. "I think Brooke and I have been able to sniff out a way around the collapsed area that will put you back into Colda's tunnel about a half mile down, and it's much closer than going back through the entrance behind the Professor House. Wish I was going along. Good luck, guys."

Stephanie bid them goodbye and said something

to Victor that made his face grave. She kissed him and gave Brooke a hug.

"Take care of my big brother for me until I get back," she whispered in her ear. "Even if he seems like he doesn't want you to."

Brooke felt as though there was much more Stephanie wanted to say, but she gave Brooke a final squeeze and departed.

Victor took the lead and they made their way to the basement, clicking on the headlamps on the helmets. She heard Tuney's breathing amp up, and she recalled his trepidation about the tunnels. She wondered if Victor had filled him in on the stranger they'd seen at the Professor House. Her own breathing accelerated a notch as the darkness swallowed up everything except the pale beams of their lamps.

Denise gasped at the pawn drawing illuminated next to the mouth of the tunnel they'd used before. "Who would have guessed it? He must not have been completely crazy."

"Crazy enough," Tuney grunted as they stopped at the pile of rubble. Footsteps sounded in the passage behind them.

Victor put a hand protectively out toward Brooke, sliding her around behind him, pulling her closer. The beam of a flashlight dazzled her eyes and she shaded her face with her hand.

Stryker emerged from the dark corner. "Ready for the second part of your tour?"

"We're retracing our steps. I want to see the room we passed last time, the circular chamber."

"Nothing to see there," he said with a shrug, "but I'll lead the way."

Victor glanced at Brooke. "Hey, Stryker, you must have a good sense of direction, being a cabbie."

"Yeah," Stryker grunted.

"I understand you drove in San Francisco, right near Brooke's father's museum."

He shrugged. "I drove a lot of places."

Victor pressed closer. "Were you there the day of the robbery?"

"No, and after that happened, the place closed up for a while so business dried up. I had to go elsewhere." He glared at Victor. "I don't have a rich family to keep me afloat, you see."

Though she wanted to ask him if he'd been in Colda's apartment the previous night, Brooke could tell that was all they were going to get out of Stryker. Likewise she could also discern that Victor was not about to give up. A confrontation would occur sometime, and it would be soon.

Stryker pushed to the front and they skirted the rubble, finding once again the small passage that led away into the smaller tube. Victor made sure they all stopped for a drink of water before they pressed in, losing no time in filing one at a time down the ladder Stryker had showed them before.

Brooke's face was sweaty in spite of the relative cool. She remembered Victor's intensity from their previous entrapment. He made sure the women and Tuney made it down the ladder before he climbed down behind them. They began the long silent march through the tunnel, pants rolled up against the ankle-deep water.

Brooke touched her aunt's hand. "I think Tad would love this adventure."

She smiled. "I think you're right."

Thoughts of her brother cheered her. She'd be back home soon, with an adventure story to tell him. She desperately hoped she would have a happy ending to their treasure hunt. A knot of worry formed again in her stomach.

Chin up.

They continued on. Up ahead at the junction of the two tunnels, they came again to the strange room, the opening of which was six feet off the floor of the tunnel. No wonder she hadn't been able to see inside. Victor's tall frame enabled him to just peek over the top and into the enclosure. Whatever he'd seen there before had made him determined to return.

Her stomach tightened.

Victor heaved himself up after a boost from Tuney. After he made it up and through the opening, he turned back and then leaned over to assist the others. When he took her hand, Brooke again felt the tingle of excitement his touch seemed to awaken in her. He helped her over the edge, pulling her against his body as he did so before he gently put her on her feet.

Pulse revving, she looked around in wonder. The

room was an oblong shape, the periphery crowded with barrels and old metal boxes.

"Some sort of bomb shelter," Brooke surmised.

"Exactly," Victor said. "They were common during the Cold War. Theory was that people would hunker down in here and be safe from the radiation. Kept them supplied with food, water, sanitary and medical supplies."

Tuney snorted. "Not exactly a long-term solution." He rolled his shoulders. "Who could live underground?"

Stryker was pacing. "So you've seen it. Let's go."

"Why so anxious?" Victor asked.

Stryker looked away. "Bad feeling here. Could be unstable."

Denise looked at the stone roof above them. "He might be right."

There were no windows leading out of the space, only a round hole about two feet across directly in the center of the ceiling, and on the floor a bundle of pipes ran the length of the space. Brooke slipped off her pack and set it down.

As she did so, she spotted a flash of red bundled between two metal casks. She pulled it out. "This certainly isn't from the Cold War era," she said, fingers sliding along the soft wool.

"This isn't either," Victor said, holding up a small paper bag and peering into the contents with his flashlight. He pulled out a small object wrapped in waxed paper.

"Someone has been living here," Brooke said in astonishment. "Colda?"

"Nah," Stryker said, kicking at a barrel. The sound echoed mournfully around the space like a funeral bell. "Probably just a bum."

"He's probably right," Denise said. "Why live in a place you know will be demolished? It must be a vagrant."

"I'll have to disagree," Victor said. With two fingertips he pulled out a half sandwich from the waxed paper. There was a look of triumph on his face when he spoke. "Half of a tomato and cheese sandwich, Colda's favorite kind. It's homemade. The cheese is only a little stale. He's been here recently."

"I don't see any stockpiles of food," Brooke said.

"He was probably hiding under the bed in the Professor House," Victor said. "He went back for supplies, and you surprised him."

Denise exhaled loudly. "He probably meant to stay out of sight until he could come back for the painting," she said, beaming her flashlight in between the barrels, voice tight with excitement. "The picture might be in here."

She began to search quickly, flashlight dancing in and out. "It's dry, not too hot. If it's packed correctly, there would be minimal damage."

Brooke heard an odd squeaking noise that seemed to be coming from the center of the room. She let the conversation drift on around her as she moved closer.

"There's no painting here," Tuney said.

"Don't have to tell me twice," Stryker said. "I'm out of here. If that crazy old man comes back, I don't wanna be anywhere close." He scrambled up to the opening and lifted himself over.

Victor made a move to stop him but Denise spoke up. "Oh, let him go. He'll wait around for us to finish searching, I'm sure."

Brooke wasn't so sure, but she was still trying to find the source of the strange noise. All at once the sound changed and a trickle of water tumbled through the hole in the ceiling.

In a matter of seconds the trickle had turned into a torrent.

Victor heard Brooke's cry mingled with the roar of water that was now pouring from the hole. "Everybody out," he yelled over the din.

Denise's face was stricken. "If it's here, it will be ruined." She splashed to the far corner, light glinting off the cascade that was now up to their shins.

"No way to save anything now," he called.

Tuney and Brooke moved toward the opening, slogging through the foaming water.

"I hate tunnels," Tuney griped.

Victor hoisted him into the opening, where he perched like a mountain goat. "No sign of Stryker. So much for a trusty guide," Tuney called down.

Victor yelled again to Denise. "Let's go. Water's risen too much to save anything even if it is here."

Denise looked as though she would ignore him but after a moment she turned and pushed to the opening, where Tuney helped her up and over. The water was moving with considerable force now, slamming at Victor's waist and continuing to rise.

He beckoned to Brooke and she moved closer until he saw her small frame stop suddenly. A look of panic crossed her face.

"Come on, Brooke," he called. "We've got to get out of here."

"I can't." Her voice was high, tight with fear. "My foot broke one of the pipes. I'm caught."

He immediately jerked off his pack, dove under the water and pulled himself closer, fighting the force that sought to push him away. Feeling his way along the pipes, he touched her hip and followed with his fingers down to her ankle. It was locked in tight between a solid pipe and the broken one. He tried to grab hold of the narrowest pipe, which felt to be nearly six inches around, but pulling did not budge it at all. He stood up and found the water was nearly up to his chest, which put it at her shoulders.

Panic began in his gut but the terror on her face made him put it aside. "I'm going to get something to pry the pipes. Hang on." He had time only to squeeze her hand once before he dove back down looking for something, anything to force the bars apart.

Some of the boxes were floating now and the water was a tumult of half-empty cans and other debris. He found nothing. Dirty water obscured his vision and he flailed around, searching with his fingers for something, anything.

His lungs screamed a complaint.

Breaking the surface again, he caught sight of Tuney's head in the opening.

"Brooke's stuck," he shouted. "Need a bar, something to pry with."

Tuney nodded and disappeared.

Victor fought his way back to Brooke, who was now up to her chin in water. He grabbed her face. "I'm going to get you out. I promise."

He saw that, in spite of the fear, she trusted him.

The deep pools of her eyes telegraphed her feelings back to him.

She trusted him.

He turned in circles. Somewhere in the disgusting mess there had to be a tool that could free her.

He dove again, clawing through the water to find anything he could use. Nothing.

Nothing.

The water was rising.

Brooke would die.

She trusted him and she would die, still trusting him as the water filled her lungs and drowned out her life.

No. God in Heaven, if You're up there, help me this time.

It was an angry prayer, filled with rage and bitterness of many long years.

His lungs burned as he ducked down again, pawing through the mess, still nothing appearing that might help until he heard Tuney shout.

"Here."

Victor grabbed the slender rod that Tuney shoved through the opening.

With one glance at Brooke, who had her chin tipped toward the ceiling as the water crested her chin, he dove down, still hearing her gasp of breath in his ears.

The rod fit between the pipes and he pushed with all his might on the other end. The pipe didn't budge. Feeling darkness crowd the edges of his vision, he pushed again with all the strength he possessed. The pipe gave a fraction of an inch.

One more push with no result.

Then Tuney was beside him, adding his weight to the rod.

A tiny give.

The pipe grudgingly moved a fraction of an inch more, enough to allow Brooke to wriggle free. When she didn't move, he realized she didn't have the strength to do so.

Or maybe it was too late.

He pulled her leg from the entrapment and propelled them both to the surface, her body limp in his arms.

SEVENTEEN

Victor and Tuney carried her over the edge and a few feet away from the tunnel entrance.

Denise's face was milk-white, hands pressed to her mouth.

He laid Brooke down in the driest spot he could find, a higher section of the uneven floor that was not yet inundated, and put his cheek to her mouth, his own heart hammering so hard he could hardly make his own senses work properly. How could it be that he could lose her?

A paralyzing horror swept through him like a wave of frigid water.

Tuney's hand gripped his shoulder so hard the fingers dug into his muscles.

He put his cheek closer, until her cold lips grazed his skin.

Then he felt it.

A whisper of breath on his face, the sweetest sensation he'd experienced in his whole life. Unable to speak or move he breathed in and out. *Thank you, thank you.* He was not sure to whom he offered the sentiment, but it flowed out of him straight from his throbbing heart. Then he turned her on her side and slid his fingers along her throat to reassure himself her pulse was still strong.

"Is she okay?" Denise whispered, dropping to her knees on the wet floor. "Please, tell me she's okay?"

Tuney released his death grip and moved to Denise. "Let him work."

Brooke coughed and water gushed from her mouth. Victor helped her sit up. The sight of her took his breath away. Never in his entire existence had he seen something so beautiful as that waterlogged woman with her hair plastered around her face and water dripping from her eyelashes.

She blinked at him and her lips broke into a sweet smile. "Thank you," she whispered, and then she began to cry.

Victor embraced her, burying his head in the wet strands of her hair, squeezing her body to his. "It's okay. You're okay." He was no longer sure if he was talking to himself or to her as his lips found the smooth skin of her neck and he felt the precious pulse beating there like the notes in an exquisite symphony.

She clung to him and he reassured her as best he could, not with words, because his own voice seemed to have failed him, but with his embrace. *You're alive,* he wanted to say. *You're alive and I'm not going to lose you.* At that moment it felt as if he had indeed taken possession of a treasure.

Her sobs gradually ebbed until he realized Denise was speaking. He pulled away and let her comfort Brooke, speaking soft words that he didn't hear. He stood and staggered back, his own legs shaky.

Tuney steadied him and they moved away a few paces.

"Close one," Tuney said. "You okay?"

Victor nodded, wiping the water from his face that was trickling down from his hair. He tried to get his brain to focus on facts. "Any sign of Stryker?"

"No." Tuney folded his hands across his chest.

"Thanks," Victor said. "For what you did back there."

Tuney shrugged. "I'm not the black-hearted rogue you think I am."

Victor was too tired to take on the conversation he needed to have with Tuney. Brooke was alive, with Tuney's help, and it was all that mattered at the moment. More than any treasure, more than vengeance. Something shifted inside him and he wished he was alone, someplace quiet and calm where he could analyze the feeling.

Instead he was in a damp tunnel growing ever damper as the water continued to spill over the side of the bomb-shelter chamber.

Tuney gazed at the tumbling water. "Funny how that water started pouring in just as we started poking around."

"Yeah, funny," Victor said. "Almost like someone opened a valve above us."

"And if someone did that, then we're definitely not alone down here."

Victor locked eyes with Tuney. "I think maybe it's time for us to go and let the cops handle this."

Tuney nodded. "Couldn't have phrased it better myself."

Victor should have felt profound disappointment, the intolerable sensation that accompanied an unmet goal. The Tarkenton, if it was hidden away, would remain that way, possibly forever. He looked at Brooke, now being cradled by her aunt, and found that the treasure didn't seem to matter anymore.

They rejoined the women. "We're going back up," Victor said. "Too dangerous down here, and Brooke needs to be taken to the hospital to be sure there's no water in her lungs."

Both women looked at him with the same expression. "But I'm okay," Brooke said, pink suffusing her cheeks. "Thanks to you two."

"Someone turned on those pipes intentionally," Tuney said. "This isn't a fun game anymore, and staying here is just inviting trouble."

Brooke got to her feet. "Mr. Tuney, it was never a game to me in the first place."

Victor moved to her. "I know. I know how much it means to you and your father, but your life means more." He held her gaze with his own.

After a long moment, she nodded. "Okay."

Denise shook her head. "You take her up, Victor. I'm going to look around some more."

"Absolutely not," he said. "We're all going."

She cocked her head. "I'm a grown woman. I can take care of myself. I've got a pack of supplies and plenty of flashlight batteries. I'll look around for a few hours and mark my way as I go. If I'm not out by morning, you can send in the troops."

Brooke put a hand on her arm. "No," she said softly. "He's right. Your safety is more important that the painting."

Denise shook her head.

Brooke seemed to snap. "Listen to me. It's a piece of canvas and some strokes of paint," she said, her voice rising with every word. "It's a painting made by a man, a regular person like you or me. It's not," she said, voice strident, "something to be worshiped more than living, breathing people." The last word echoed throughout the tunnel.

Victor saw in her face she was no longer talking just about the Tarkenton. Her eyes revealed a deep longing probably born from many years of living with a parent who was passionate to the point of mania about art. He'd encountered people like that often in his line of work, people desperate to own masterpieces, even illegally, even if it meant locking them away in dark rooms where no one would ever see.

"It's all your father has," Denise said, her voice breaking. "I've got to help him."

"No," Brooke cried. "He has you and me and Tad."

Victor wondered if that would be enough to sustain Donald through the newest round of investigation. What was more, Victor was reminded he would do everything in his power to see the old man punished. He shifted uneasily.

Brooke's anger seemed to drain away all at once. "Please, Aunt Denise," she said softly. "Let's get out of here and go back home."

The words stabbed at Victor.

Go back home.

Walk away from the treasure.

From him.

What other choice did she have?

Denise considered for another moment. She let out a long, defeated sigh. "Okay, honey. Of course you're right. Let's go."

Tuney shouldered his pack, a bemused expression on his face. Victor took the flashlight from his back pocket, which had mercifully survived the drenching, and they began the long walk back to the ladder.

Tuney kept glancing over his shoulder. "Wonder where Stryker took himself off to."

Victor wondered, also. Brooke and Denise followed behind him in silence. The water on the floor of the tunnel still trickled along, dampening their already soaked shoes and pant legs. Victor was cold so he knew Brooke must be even more so.

He hurried his pace. Something coiled inside him. A sense of tension that seemed to increase with every passing moment. Was it the realization that he and Brooke were hours away from going their separate ways? The knowledge that Treasure Seekers had failed to complete their task?

He chose to put away the thoughts in favor of action and pressed even faster until he reached the bottom of the ladder. Without his headlamp, which had washed away in his effort to save Brooke, he could see only blackness above him as he began the climb.

The clang of his feet on the ladder sounded loud in the confines of the tunnel. An occasional grumbled complaint from Tuney floated up to him, and some soothing remark from Brooke. How could she still be the comforter? After everything that had happened?

He forced himself, hand over hand, until he felt the air change, warming up several degrees.

"Couple more feet," he called back behind him.

"Swell," Tuney snapped, "because my clothes are sticking to me like a second skin."

He continued up until he saw something that made his heart speed up and his feet stop at the same moment.

"What is it?" Brooke said, her head bumping his calf. "Why did you stop?"

He didn't answer at first, just moved up another rung and stretched out his flashlight to be sure. The metal clanged like a gong.

He pocketed the flashlight and applied his shoulder to the obstruction before he called back to the others. "The opening is locked. Somebody's slid the grate back over the top and secured it somehow. It won't budge."

"I can't believe it," Brooke said.

"I can," Tuney growled. "Why would our luck change now?"

Brooke tugged on his pant leg. "You're going to break a bone. We've got to go back down."

Victor nodded and they descended.

At the bottom, Tuney flicked his light on and beamed it around.

Brooke gasped. "My aunt is gone."

After a second of shock, the two men jogged down the tunnel, past the flooded room. It didn't take long before they turned around and Victor followed Tuney back, dread bunching in his gut. "No sign of her."

Brooke stared. "She must have gotten lost, disoriented." She realized as she spoke that it was not the truth.

Tuney's scowl was deeper than ever. "She dropped back behind us on purpose. She can't give up on that Tarkenton."

Brooke groaned. "We've got to get help and find her."

"Well, we're not getting out that way," Victor said, gesturing to the blocked passageway.

"Had to be Stryker that locked it," Tuney said.

"Doesn't accomplish much." Victor rubbed at his shoulder. "He can keep us down here for a while, but eventually my sister and brother will come looking, or Lock will send the cops."

Tuney's eyes narrowed.

"You don't think Lock will send the police?" Brooke asked.

Tuney didn't answer.

Victor beamed a flashlight ahead. "She can't have gotten far, and we don't have much choice here. We wait by the ladder for what could be hours, knowing that there's probably someone loose who doesn't want us down here."

"Someone who might be deranged professor Leo Colda," Tuney added.

"Or we go after her," Victor said.

Brooke shifted impatiently. "I say we go, and quickly. We're wasting time."

Tuney sighed. "I don't suppose you have any idea where this tunnel leads?"

"No," Victor said. "But wherever it goes it will give us plenty of time for you to explain."

"Explain what?" Brooke asked.

Victor started down the tunnel. "Explain why he's lying."

Brooke hurried to keep up. "Lying about what?"

"Tuney wasn't hired by the university to look for Professor Colda. Steph uncovered that tidbit and told me right before we came down here." Though he kept his tone casual, Victor's question was deadly serious. "Since we find ourselves all alone with time on our hands, this seems like an opportune moment. Who do you really work for, Mr. Tuney?"

EIGHTEEN

The silence thickened between them as Victor watched Tuney's face, the beetled brows, the eyes glinting in the gloom.

Tuney hesitated. "In the process of investigating the theft four years ago, I met all the players—Lock, Donald, the security guards, everyone. I kept on it, as you know, over the years because I had a feeling I could find proof that Ramsey did it."

"For the reward," Brooke said bitterly.

He sighed. "That would be a sweet payoff, but it's more the kind of person I am. Ex-cop and all that."

"Fired cop," Victor added.

"Yeah, fired for helping myself to a little rent money off a guy who made ten grand a day selling drugs. He deals drugs, I'm a cop with alimony payments and a cheap Datsun. Who gets punished?"

"How do we know that's the truth?" Victor asked.

"I guess you don't."

"So how did you come to be involved in this case?"

"I got a call from Lock that Ramsey had shipped a painting to Colda."

"That's interesting," Brooke cut in. "Dean Lock said he wasn't sure my father ever really sent a painting in the first place."

"Lock knew. He remembered my name from the museum fiasco so he called me up. I told you I've always been eager to dig into Donald's life a little deeper. I put Fran on the case, and she followed Brooke. I stayed on the trail after Colda."

Victor continued on into the darkness, slowed by piles of rock and broken pipes littering the floor. "Did Lock specifically mention the Tarkenton?"

"Not specifically. He said he thought Ramsey might have sent one of the stolen museum sketches to Colda to be fenced or sold. Wanted me to prove it. Then when Colda went missing, he wanted me to find him."

Brooke stopped dead. "So all this time you've been working for Lock to prove my father guilty?"

"That's what I thought."

"What do you mean?" Victor said.

"Some things didn't add up."

"Like what?"

"Little things. Lock said he barely knew Colda, but I hear he's been playing chess with the guy on and off for years. He said he'd never been in Colda's apartment, but I got the impression the place had been searched before I got there, before the police had been notified. Small stuff, but enough to get me thinking."

Victor turned it over in his mind. He hadn't trusted Lock from the start, but he had only Tuney's word against the dean's, and Tuney hadn't been forthcoming either. "So you were directed to follow us along in the tunnels in case we found one of the stolen pieces."

"Or some clue to Colda's whereabouts."

"Did Colda fake his own death because he knew Lock was onto him?"

"Could be."

They stopped short as the passage split into two. Shining their lights down both did nothing to help them decide on a direction. No sound indicated which way Denise might have gone. Each direction stretched out before them, dark and still. The tunnels could lead them farther and farther away from an exit, or closer to another near disaster. Brooke shivered, and without thinking, Victor put an arm around her, chafing some warmth back into her body.

He spread the map out against the tunnel wall. "Steph marked some possible routes, as best she could. I'd guess the left-hand passage winds under the admin offices and toward the Professor House. The right hand is more of a mystery."

Brooke stood again, hands outstretched. "Is it my imagination or is the left-hand tunnel warmer than the right?"

Victor laughed. "You're getting good at this tunnel

exploration business. Yes, warmer on the left. Drier, too, higher than the other."

"I vote for exploring the warm and dry route first." He was glad to see that she still had a spot for humor in spite of the worry he saw in her face.

"I'm sure your aunt is fine. We'll find her," he said quietly. *Hopefully before she runs into Stryker or Colda.*

They decided on the left-hand passage, which Victor carefully marked with a can of spray paint from Tuney's pack. All his supplies were underwater in the bomb shelter, and even his flashlight was starting to lose power. Brooke's stores were also underwater back in the bomb shelter, so like it or not, Tuney was the best supplied of the group. Tuney pulled out a box of animal crackers and handed them each a palmful.

"Animal crackers?" Victor said.

"I like animal crackers," Tuney huffed. "They're good for energy and they don't take up much space. If you have something else in your pockets, feel free to pass."

Victor felt slightly ridiculous eating the animal crackers, but they did take the edge off his hunger, along with the bottle of water Tuney produced for him and Brooke to share as they trekked along for the better part of an hour. The tunnel narrowed until they were forced to walk single file, avoiding the pipes that ran overhead radiating enough heat to make them sweat.

"Careful not to touch them," Victor warned. "They're hot enough to burn."

A skittering along the walls startled him.

Tuney snorted. "More rats. This place keeps getting better and better."

In fact, it grew darker and hotter. Their clothes were nearly dry. Another hour of walking, and he could feel Brooke beginning to lag behind. "Let's rest," he said. They sat on the floor, sharing the last of the water bottle. Tuney settled with a grunt near them.

Above was a series of pipes covered in chipped red-and-blue paint. A network of wires webbed the ceiling, as well, some chewed through by the rats, Victor guessed. The floor bore traces of rodent droppings, but at least it was dry. Above them, about every four feet or so, was a dark hole, covered by a rusted grate, like a series of dark eyes peering down at them. His skin prickled and he felt the sensation of being watched. It was probably his imagination due to what Brooke had mentioned earlier, but nonetheless he kept a wary eye out as Brooke closed her eyes and leaned her head against the wall behind her.

Victor checked his phone, a useless gesture as it had been soaked recently. He wouldn't get a signal anyway. Fortunately, his watch still functioned. "Just after noon. Luca's plane should have landed. They'll be on their way back soon."

"What if they go back to the office?" Tuney said.

"They'll come here."

"How do you know?"

"Because I know my brother. He'll want in on the action as soon as he possibly can manage it."

Brooke gave him a wan smile and he was glad his remark had cheered her. Inside he felt more concerned than he let on. His brother and sister would find the blocked tunnel fairly quickly, but it might take them some time to get through. In the meantime, Denise was still nowhere in sight and Brooke was looking more and more fatigued. The walls were closing in on Tuney, from the look of the man. He rocked back and forth, the glint of his silvered hair eerie.

"What am I doing here?" he mumbled, jerking at the sound of a rat scuttling along the pipes overhead. "Never should have joined up with this insanity."

"Beginning to think it wasn't worth what Lock is paying you?"

Tuney glared at him. "I told you I can't let things go, even if I wanted to. If Lock has been playing me, then he'll pay for it."

Victor pitied him in that moment until he came to the uncomfortable realization that he was not altogether different than the doggedly determined Tuney. Determination had allowed him to be a great doctor at one point in his life, and a successful treasure hunter. And it had kept the injustice of Jennifer's death burning in his chest for four years. There would be no relief, no quenching of that inexhaustible flame until Donald Ramsey paid for what he did.

He found Brooke watching him, her eyes shadowed with fatigue. He wished he did not feel strange when he gazed back into those blue eyes, off-balance and uneasy, filled with the insane need to crush her close and leave her breathless.

Tuney leaped to his feet so suddenly Brooke cried out. He spun around, wielding the flashlight like a weapon before he slumped back against the wall. "Just the rats. They're fighting over something in the corner."

Victor walked closer and the rats scattered. One big hairy rodent with a mottled tail glared at Victor, his prize clenched tightly between yellowed incisors before scampering away into the darkened recesses behind the pipes.

"Brooke, what did Denise put in her pack to eat?"

Brooke joined him, hand on his shoulder to look past. "Your sister gave us packages of dried fruit. Why?"

"Because I just watched the head rat scamper away with a bag of dried apricots."

For a moment, Brooke's heart could not seem to figure out what to feel until one overwhelming thought rose to the top.

Hurry.

Like the crush of water she'd felt before, the impulse to find her aunt and get out of the tunnels rushed wildly inside. "She came this way. We're close." Brooke started down the passage, heedless of the fact that she had only a small penlight loaned to her by Tuney. Victor caught her arm and pulled her to him. "Careful, the pipes."

She felt the heat not from the metal conduits, but a delicious warmth trickling through her body where it made contact with his. He murmured in her ear again, which sent a network of sparks down her side. "Let me go first."

She acquiesced, as much to get her nerves in check as anything else. Tuney seemed relieved to be moving again as he brought up the rear. The passage grew lower until Victor had to hunch over to continue on.

A pitiful wail echoed through the tunnel causing them to stop dead.

Tuney wiped a hand over his face. "Man or woman?"

"Can't tell," Victor said. "Which direction?"

They waited. Brooke's heart pounded so forcefully she was not sure she could hear anything until the wail came again from somewhere ahead of them. "Leave me be," it shrieked, making the hair on the back of her neck prickle. So distorted was the voice that she was not able to tell if it was her aunt.

"Whoever it is, they need help," she said, pushing ahead of Victor and moving as fast as she could up the tunnel. A strange flickering light appeared ahead. It must be Denise's lantern. She ran, the light gradually illuminating another chamber, again set high in the wall. A pile of stones on the tunnel floor provided an easy step up into the chamber. She had not quite crested the top when there was a deafening explosion, the sound of a gun firing.

Ears ringing, she found herself pulled back as Victor grabbed her around the waist and hauled her into the shelter of a brace of pipes. Panic seized her. "My aunt. Colda shot her," she panted, clapping her hands over her mouth to contain the scream that threatened to bubble up.

He squeezed her shoulder. "We'll help. Stay here. Please." His look calmed her, momentarily overcoming the terror in her gut. What would they find in the chamber? Thoughts crowded into her head leaving her dizzy with horror, terror as bad as she'd felt when she'd been close to drowning.

Victor and Tuney took up positions on either side of the gap. Tuney took the lead now, gesturing to Victor silently that they would go on three. He stabbed a finger in the air to count. One. Her breath caught.

Two.

Was the shooter still on the other side, waiting to catch the two men in the crossfire? She couldn't stand it. Crawling out from behind the pipes she screamed, "No, wait!"

Too late.

Tuney used the piles of stones and popped up, giving him a view of the space while Victor, keeping low, looked over.

She heard his intake of breath.

And then he was up and over the opening, followed by Tuney.

Her body went rigid, waiting for another shot, but there was only a faint scuffling from inside. Darting to the opening, she climbed on the step and peered in.

A body lay on the floor in the farside of the chamber, hidden by shadows.

Fear clawed at her insides and the room swam before her eyes. Forcing her legs to keep moving, she climbed up and over, ignoring the scrape of brick against her shins. She wanted to run, to see who it was lying there under Victor's ministrations, but her feet would not cooperate. The best she could do was stand there, horror prickling through her body, until Tuney noticed her and nudged Victor. He moved slightly and she saw that it was not her aunt but Stryker who lay on the floor, face pale and blood leaking from his side.

She ran now, crossing the floor and kneeling next to Victor.

Stryker was alive, his eyelids fluttering open and closed, dirt streaking his dark skin. She found his hand and held it, squeezing the fingers, which were still mercifully warm.

Victor's face was grave. Tuney offered him a small first-aid kit and he ripped it open, using the scissors to slit Stryker's shirt.

Stryker moaned as he applied pressure.

"Can you talk?" Brooke asked, leaning close. "What happened? Who did this to you?"

But Stryker did not look at Brooke. His eyes were riveted instead on Victor. "I'm sorry," he said, his voice a whisper.

Victor didn't answer. His concentration was on the wound he was treating. Stryker reached his free hand and grabbed Victor's jacket. "I'm sorry, man. I wanted to get back to my girl, you know? To have a start for us. That's all it was. Being a cabbie didn't pay enough and I had the chance to make a big score."

Victor stopped as if he'd been slapped. "What are you sorry for?"

"I didn't think anyone would get hurt," he mumbled. His face twitched in pain.

Victor leaned close to Stryker's face. "Tell me what you did, Stryker."

Stryker groaned and his eyes closed, tears leaking out and streaking through the grime on his face. Victor tried to rouse him with a gentle shake to his shoulders.

Stryker remained unconscious.

Brooke's heart was in her throat as Victor checked him over. "He's alive, and I think the bullet missed any organs, but he's bleeding heavily. I'll try to stop it, but he won't be able to stay down here long."

Brooke handed Victor a roll of bandages and continued to stroke Stryker's arm. What had he just confessed to? There was no gun around, Tuney had checked thoroughly while Brooke watched, so the gunshot was not self-inflicted.

"No sign of the shooter," Tuney said as he returned from the outer corridor.

"And no sign of my aunt?"

"No," Tuney said.

Brooke caught the tone in his answer. "Before you start spinning theories about any more members of my family, my aunt did not shoot Stryker. First off, she'd have no reason to, and second, she had no gun. I watched her fill her pack. Are you satisfied?"

Tuney shrugged. "That leaves Colda, or some other psychopath who happens to be wandering the tunnels."

Brooke suppressed a shiver. *Just keep out of sight, Denise, until we get to you.* She took a moment to examine the bomb shelter. This one was empty of supplies, just a bare circular chamber with the holes set halfway up the walls.

Much better if the place floods, she thought grimly, willing away the memory of her near drowning.

When Victor finished applying the bandages, he sat back, exchanging a look with Tuney before unrolling the map again.

"One of us has to get out of here or at least get to a spot where we can call for help. Stryker's going to need an ambulance. We don't have the luxury of waiting for my brother and sister anymore."

Tuney shook his head. "I'll go."

Brooke heard Victor grind his teeth before he turned to her, moving her away to the farside of the chamber. His face was grim. "I think you should go with Tuney. I don't entirely trust him, but you'd be safer than staying here."

"I'm not going."

His hands fisted. "This isn't the time for stubbornness. Someone is likely to die down here."

"Then I have to make sure it isn't my aunt." She thought to herself, *or you.*

"Brooke," he started.

"Listen to me. It's not about the painting anymore, or my father or anything else. It's about that poor man there, hurt and possibly dying, and my aunt who needs rescuing whether she knows it or not. I'm staying."

An arrogant look flashed across his face. "I don't need any more patients to treat."

"I promise I will do my best not to become one."

"That's not it."

She crossed her arms. "This whole thing has been about family to me and you happen to hate my family."

He caught her by the shoulders. "You know that isn't true."

"Isn't it?" She looked deep into his eyes. "Hasn't the last four years been about punishing my father?"

He looked away. "It was about finding justice."

"You know what? I'd sure like to find some justice, too, to let the world know the truth about my father. You want to destroy him. My aunt and I want to save him. Pardon me if I don't want to leave my family affairs in your hands."

His mouth closed in a taut line. "Fine. Stay if you want to."

"I will," she said softly.

He moved closer, gliding his fingers along her arms, sending ripples of sweetness surging through her. Why did her body not understand what her mind grasped completely?

"But I'm not out to ruin your family. I just..." Victor started.

Tuney cleared his throat. "Don't mean to interrupt, but I've got a long walk ahead through rats, shooters, floods and who knows what else, to find a way out that may or may not exist. Seems like I'd better get started."

Victor pulled away, leaving Brooke slightly dizzy. He and Tuney scanned the map while Brooke knelt next to Stryker. She took off her jacket and wadded it up under his head as a makeshift pillow and then held his hand and prayed for him.

She looked at the lines of pain around his mouth that even unconsciousness could not erase, and thought about his strange confession.

Oh, Stryker. What have you done?

NINETEEN

Victor and Tuney identified the direction that might be most likely to provide a way out near the Professor House. Tuney gave them a sloppy salute and said in his best John Wayne voice, "Until we meet again, partner."

Then he was gone. Victor began to pace, following the periphery of the room, which was mercifully dry and warm but not dangerously so. There were broken bricks on the floor, the only objects in the bare chamber with its cold stone floor and low ceiling. Six-inch holes were set ink-dark into the walls. The only light came from his failing flashlight and Brooke's penlight.

"We should conserve the batteries," he said, flicking his off and activating a light stick that Tuney had given him before he left. Brooke silently switched off her penlight and they sat next to Stryker, bathed in the otherworldly glow of the light stick.

The silence grew between them. That was fine with Victor. His mouth would not cooperate when

Brooke was around, insisting on saying things without the consent of his brain. Why did he forget all thoughts of treasure and vengeance now that she was sitting next to him? What happened to his orderly, meticulously reasoned arguments when her hair brushed his cheek with a satin tickle? He checked his watch, willing Tuney to hurry, or his brother and sister to make it through the grate.

When the feel of her next to him made his senses too jumbled, he busied himself tending to Stryker, checking his pulse and wishing again they had at least a blanket to wrap around him.

"I wonder what he meant," Brooke said softly.

"I wish I knew." Victor yearned to pace, but it was too dark now to move anywhere safely.

She startled him with the next question. "Who are Pearson, Jackney and Rivera? The names you mentioned when we were trapped in that hot room."

"Patients," he growled, looking away.

"What happened to them?"

"They died."

She didn't answer, just looked at him, and before he realized it the words were tumbling from his mouth.

"They died, but they shouldn't have. I'd lost patients before over the course of my career and after them, of course, but I knew why. Sometimes they were too weak to survive the surgery or infection set in, et cetera. But those three…" He pulled out his wallet and took out a small piece of paper, worn and creased from use, with the three names written on it. "I could not understand why they died. Every day I searched for the answer, researched and went through their medical histories, the moment by moment of the surgery, but I never could figure it out."

Brooke reached for his hand. "Some things you don't get to know."

He felt a surge of anger as he pulled out of reach. "That's it? That's the answer? Some things just happen and I don't get to know or understand why? I just have to accept it, to know that I'm not good enough or smart enough or—" he searched for the word "—or worthy enough to know why?"

She nodded.

"And you accept that? After your father destroyed you and you lost the dream of becoming a dancer. You just accept that it's not for you to understand why."

"Yes."

"I can't be complacent like that. I'm not that kind of person."

"Not complacent. Angry, hurt, disappointed, enraged, sorrowful, Victor. All those things, but hopeful, too, because I know there's something better the Lord has in mind." She smiled. "He's smarter than me." Stryker stirred and she moved to him and took his hand.

"Why do you pray for him?" Victor snapped. "He's no innocent."

"Neither am I," Brooke said.

"He's probably a criminal."

"Like Stephanie?"

He stiffened. "My sister made some mistakes, huge mistakes, but she's past that."

"Huge mistakes, but you love her anyway."

"Of course. She's my sister."

"So you care for her even though she disappointed you and let you down?"

He waved the question away. "Of course."

She turned to him. "And that is exactly the way I feel about my father, and I'm going to continue to pray for him, and for Stryker." Her voice dropped to a murmur. "And for you, Victor, because you might never know why those men died." She added softly, "Or Jennifer."

He stared at her, breath held until his body forced his lungs to start up again. "I can't accept that."

"It helps when you know that there's a God up there who loves you. He's in charge and you're not. It's a comfort, actually."

A rat skittered across the pipe over their heads.

A comfort. To believe. How could she embrace something that ridiculously simple?

He got to his feet, shoved the paper back into his pocket and checked on Stryker again.

Stryker moaned and Victor tried to pour a little water from their scant supply into his mouth. He coughed and his eyes flicked open.

"Is she dead?" Stryker croaked. "I didn't mean to kill them."

"Who?" Victor said, his ear close to Stryker's mouth.

"Shot was supposed to scare her. I'm a bad shot. I hate guns." His breathing grew shallow. "Bad driver, too. Bad everything. Couldn't even tail you on my motorcycle."

"Did you shoot the woman at my office building?" Victor pressed. "Why would you do that?"

Stryker closed his eyes and fell back into a semi-conscious state. Victor stood, frustration and a growing sense of anxiety prickling his body. "He must have killed Fran."

Brooke's hands were oddly luminous as she wiped Stryker's tearstained cheeks. "He said *them*. More than one."

Shock crashed through him. *I'm a bad driver.* "He apologized to me specifically."

Her eyes met his and he looked away from the horror he saw there.

"Stryker was the one who crashed into our car." Victor looked down at the prostrate figure. "Stryker is the man who killed my wife."

Brooke's head spun. "At the museum all those years ago, Stryker was driving the getaway car? Why did he come to San Francisco?"

Victor's voice was hard. "I don't know." He bumped against a protruding piece of cement.

"Sit down, Victor," she pleaded. "Let's try to figure it out."

Victor shook his head, head tilted to the ceiling, eyes closed. "As soon as you walked into Treasure Seekers I had the feeling these cases were connected."

She was unsure what to say. Though she knew deep down her father was not involved with Stryker, any mention of his name would just inflame Victor. She saw the anguish on his face and it bit at her heart.

"What really kills me," he said, voice tight, "is that I don't feel any relief. I thought once I knew, once I could look into the face of the person that ran into us and took off..." His voice trailed away.

She stood, ignoring all common sense, and put her arms around him. "I'm sorry."

He clung to her, brushing his lips to her neck, his embrace pulling her tight to his chest. She might have imagined it but she thought she felt the anger ease, a gentleness stealing into his touch as he stroked her hair.

"Brooke, you should be someone I hate. I'm black or white. You're an enemy or a friend, and I thought you were in the other camp."

"But you don't? Hate me, I mean?"

He didn't answer, just pulled her tighter to him and sighed deeply, a sound that shivered through the deepest parts of her.

She wanted to show him with her embrace that he didn't have to live in such an unforgiving world.

There were so many shades of color, so many glorious tints to experience besides his harsh black-and-white reality.

Though she longed to stay there, tucked into his embrace, he pulled away.

Only a few feet separated them, but the distance felt like miles. His expression was suddenly distant, shuttered.

She lowered herself to the floor, thoughts spinning through her mind so quickly she could hardly catch hold of them. She guessed Colda had shot Stryker, and if they didn't find her aunt soon, the same thing would happen to her.

Her stomach writhed. How long would it be before Tuney returned with help or Stephanie and Luca forced their way in? She leaned her head back against the wall and squeezed her arms around herself, feeling a draft on her neck coming from the holes bored into the concrete.

She heard a groan, which she took to be Victor until she saw him staring at her.

Had it been Stryker?

She started to go to him, when a hand came from one of the holes and seized her hair.

"Go away," a voice hissed. "Leave me be, do you hear me? Leave me be."

Victor ran to her as she tried to yank away, the viselike grip on her hair unrelenting, long fingernails digging into her scalp.

"Stop," Victor yelled. "Colda, let go." He tried to pry at the fingers wound tightly in her hair.

The hand continued to pull so hard tears sprang up in Brooke's eyes until she cried out. Victor scanned frantically. "There's got to be a passage just on the other side. Hang on." He ran from the room.

Brooke kept trying to twist away. "Please, Professor Colda, you're hurting me. I'm Donald Ramsey's daughter. You are my father's friend."

The grip loosened slightly. "They're going to kill me," the voice wailed.

"No. No, I'll help you. We can get you out of here safely." The tears made it nearly impossible to see, but she heard the voice soften.

"Tell them to stay away. If they come near me, I'll kill them. I have to." There was a half sob and suddenly she was freed so quickly she fell to her knees.

If they come near me, I'll kill them.

Colda was insane. She heard it in the panted words hissing through the hole. Anyone who approached him would be in danger. Colda had a gun.

Terror ran rampant through her veins. She raced out of the passageway. "Victor," she yelled. "Come back." The hallway was black but she didn't dare turn around. Pressing her hands to the wall, she moved in the direction she decided he must have taken. Palms scraping the roughened rock, she pushed along, stumbling and banging her shins on protruding rock. Ahead she could see nothing. Eyes searching the darkness, she tried to discover some hidden passage that she'd missed. After several more minutes, she retraced her steps. This time, she found it. A hole about four feet square cut into the rock. Warm air emanated from the hole. Victor must have crawled into it. There was no other possibility.

The idea of entering that hole made her skin clammy, but she had to warn him. Lowering herself gingerly to her hands and knees, she started in, ignoring the rock scraping through her jeans.

She had to get to Victor.

Her ankle was seized by a rough hand.

She screamed, pulling and kicking.

A deep voice yelled something which she could not understand in her fear.

Kicking desperately, she tried to push herself away, scrabbling and clawing at the rock.

She felt herself being pulled away. "Victor," she screamed. Clawing her fingers, she held tight to a jutting rock until she could hold on no longer.

The grip tightened around her ankles and she was pulled back into the tunnel.

Brooke felt a scream building inside but the shock of landing on the tunnel floor took her breath away. A big, familiar-looking man knelt next to her.

"Sorry for the rough landing. You okay?" the man said.

He had Victor's green eyes but a broader frame

and fair hair. She nodded, trying to get her breath. "Luca?"

He nodded. "Stephanie is waiting for the paramedics. We broke through the grate to get down here and found the gunshot victim. Where's Victor?"

Brooke forced a calm tone she did not feel. "He's gone after Colda."

Luca's fair eyebrows zinged upward. "Crazy professor Colda? He's really alive?"

"Yes, and I think he shot Stryker, the man you found. Victor's gone after him."

Luca didn't waste a minute. He pushed by Brooke and worked his head and shoulders into the tunnel, grunting as he did so. After a moment he groaned. "I'm too big. I can't fit." He pulled back out with a look of exasperation. Brooke got the feeling if there was a crowbar handy he would try to knock down the stone.

"I'm going to help him," she said, but Luca caught her arm.

"Not safe."

"Now you sound just like your brother. I'm going."

Luca looked helplessly around for another solution. Brooke didn't give him the chance to delay her any longer. She darted past him and scooted into the tunnel, hearing his exclamation of disapproval. It didn't matter. She had to get to Victor. Colda used to be her father's friend, and she knew she could talk him out of hurting Victor if she got the chance.

She crawled over the uneven rock, wondering how Victor had managed to scrunch his tall frame in the confined space. Damp soaked into the knees of her pants, blood oozed from scrapes on her fingers and wrists.

Ahead she thought she heard someone cry out. She hurried as fast as she could until she almost fell through a gap in the tunnel floor. Looking down she could see only a faint glow, but there was no sound.

Her breath was loud and harsh in her own ears. The heat wafted up from the space below, bringing with it the smell of mold. *Victor, where are you?*

Perhaps there was another way, another passage. She climbed carefully over the gap and continued on a few yards until she came to a bricked-off wall. Dead end. Victor must be back there, back in the lower chamber. She returned to the edge of the gap, listening intently once again.

Silence.

She found a pebble and dropped it down into the opening. It plinked against the floor quickly, telling her the floor wasn't more than six feet below.

She listened again.

More silence, then a slight scraping noise, like the sound of a heavy bundle being pulled across the floor.

A heavy bundle.

Heavy, like a dead weight.

Her insides were screaming at her to leave, go back and wait for help.

But her heart was telling her something entirely different.

Victor was down there. Maybe hurt. Maybe dead. "Lord, help me," she breathed.

Slowly, as quietly as she could, she sat on the edge of the opening and dangled her legs into the gap. The air shivered up at her, warm, too warm, black as oil and quiet as the grave. After a deep breath, Brooke dropped down into the darkness.

TWENTY

Victor was so intent on the man in front of him, he didn't hear Brooke until she stepped close enough for the lantern on the floor to illuminate her.

"Brooke," he said, both exasperated and oddly pleased to have her there. "I'd like you to meet Leo Colda."

Colda sat on a chunk of cement, his face pale and despondent. His clothes were soiled and a scrape on his cheek was angry and swollen. A slight man, he sat with his knees nearly drawn up to his chin, arms folded around his legs. He peered at Brooke as if he couldn't quite place her.

Brooke pressed her fingers to Victor's arm. "Your brother's here. They're tending to Stryker."

Victor laughed. "And Luca couldn't fit through the tunnel?"

She nodded.

"I'm surprised he isn't hacking away at the cement."

"There wasn't a crowbar handy."

Victor felt his muscles relax for the first time since

they'd started the whole adventure that morning. "I was just asking the professor why he shot Stryker."

Colda started. "They're after me. They want the painting."

Brooke moved closer. "You mean my father's painting?"

He peered at her and blinked. "You're Ramsey's daughter?"

"Yes. Professor, why did you take my father's painting?"

He rocked back and forth. "They were after it."

"Who?"

"All of them. I turned on the water to flush them out."

Victor whistled. "So Tuney was right. You nearly drowned Brooke."

Colda sighed. "The dean came to visit when he heard a package arrived from Donald. He saw it, the Tarkenton, and he knew right away, just like I did, and he wanted it for himself."

Victor heard Brooke's sharp intake of breath. "He knew that it was authentic?"

Colda nodded. "I was running tests, but it was a formality. I had to hide it until I could get it back to Donald, but the kid came after me."

"So you shot him," Victor said, watching Colda squirm back and forth.

"No. He tried to shoot me but I spun away and the bullet got him."

"Ricochet, probably." Victor locked eyes with Colda. "Where is the gun now?"

Colda shrugged. "I took it and ran." He patted his pockets. "I must have dropped it somewhere."

Brooke edged closer and crouched down next to Colda. Victor tried to give her a warning look—*he might be lying. Colda could still have the gun on him somewhere*—but she paid him no attention.

"Professor Colda, did you really steal those paintings from my father's museum like you said in the suicide note?"

Colda's face went wild, eyes popping.

From above them, someone called out. "Brooke? Are you down there?"

"Aunt Denise," Brooke cried. She ran to the opening and called up to her. "Are you okay?"

"I'm banged up, but all right."

"Hey," Victor shouted as Colda bolted to his feet and careened toward an opening Victor had not noticed. "Stop."

He grabbed the lantern and took off after Colda. Brooke yelled something to her aunt and then he heard her start down the passage behind him. Pipes crowded the ceiling above them and his senses pricked at him, trying to send him a message.

He was so occupied trying to hold the lantern and avoid the piles of fallen rock on the floor that he paid no heed at first.

"Colda," he yelled at the darting figure. "It's over. You've got to stop running. Let us help you."

Colda didn't stop.

Wires brushed Victor's face and he pushed them aside.

Again the odd sense that something was amiss floated into his mind.

Brooke panted behind him, adding her plea. "Please, Professor Colda. We can help you try to make amends."

"Stay away," Colda screamed. "Stay away from me. They're after me. They're going to kill me."

He vanished around a sharp turn and the odor became unmistakable.

Gas.

Victor stopped abruptly. "Gas leak," he called as loudly as he could. "Get out." He turned to grab Brooke but she had no time to slow and she plowed into him. The old lantern sailed out of his hand and arced through the air, smashing into the cement behind them.

They had only a split second.

He pulled on her arm and they ran farther up the tunnel as the gas ignited. The explosion ripped through the tunnel, illuminating everything in a blaze of white-hot fire that moved toward like them a hungry beast. Ahead was no shelter, no place to escape the fury that was almost upon them.

Except for one dark circle set into the floor.

He didn't slow. They ran to the hole, leaping down into it as the heat began to scorch Victor's skin.

He crushed her body to his, trying to pull her

as far down into the space as he could, feeling the molten cloud of fire pass over them, with a deafening whoosh.

The sound vibrated through him like thunder.

And then it was quiet.

Brooke did not move in his arms.

He allowed himself to imagine it only for a moment.

What if those blue eyes did not open?

If the fire had burned away her life?

His hands began to tremble and he stroked her hair, which was now hot to the touch.

"Brooke," he whispered. "Brooke."

She took a slow, shuddering breath and he felt a flood of great joy that filled him completely. He held her for a long time, until she lifted her head and looked at him.

"Are we alive?" she whispered.

"As far as I can tell," he whispered back, kissing the tip of her nose.

They struggled to their feet in what turned out to be a long cement chute, opening onto yet another tunnel. Brooke shook bits of cement from her hair. "My aunt?"

"I'm sure she's fine. My brother will find her." Victor pulled the flashlight from his pocket. The beam was faint, but it allowed him to make out the way ahead of them.

"I can see where Colda went. The dust is disturbed along this path. He's trying to escape."

"Or going after the painting."

Victor pointed the beam back up the chute. "We can't go back that way, so I guess we have no choice but to follow Colda."

"Do you think we can catch him?"

"There's still a chance."

Her eyes were shadowed. "Victor, I don't care about that painting. I just want to find him so he can clear my father. Are you willing to help me do that?"

He looked at her, ready with a neutral comment or practical remark. His mind came up with something completely different. He wanted to tell her, to give voice to the incomprehensible feelings in his soul, which had started in the flooded room and come into full flower as he'd felt her breath on his neck, but he could not. "Let's go," he said, turning from the questioning look on her face.

They picked their way along, climbing over rocks, avoiding dangling wires. Brooke was completely disoriented. She had no idea if they were still under the university or if the tunnels had led them miles away. So many questions would remain unanswered if they didn't prevent Colda's escape. Part of her was afraid of the answers he might give.

What would happen to her and Tad if Colda did not clear her father's name? Victor's hand grasped hers as he guided her around an uneven pile of broken cement chunks. His touch drove the fears away, the memory of his sheltering embrace tugged at her.

He'll be gone soon, Brooke. Just as soon as you

get out of these horrible tunnels, he'll walk out of your life.

She packed the thoughts away and focused on picking her way over the rocks. A sound from behind them caught her attention.

Victor heard it, too. They stopped and held the flashlight up. Their light was met with another as a figure moved closer through the darkness.

Denise's face went from tentative to joyful when she saw Brooke. She wrapped her in a hug. "I thought the explosion might have…" She squeezed harder and Brooke hugged her back with abandon.

"Where were you?"

"Completely lost, I'm embarrassed to say," Denise replied.

"How did you get down here?" Brooke managed.

"Victor's brother fixed a rope for me."

Brooke smiled.

"And he's really mad that he can't get his big shoulders through," Stephanie said as she joined them.

Victor kissed his sister and squeezed her tight. "Stryker?"

"Paramedics are loading him now. Cops are figuring out how to get down here and help us."

Brooke felt a surge of relief.

Stephanie surveyed the tunnel. "We're still on Colda's trail?"

Denise sighed. "He's a tenacious little guy. I don't

know why I thought I could find him or the painting by wandering around on my own."

Brooke told her what Colda said about Lock.

Denise's eyes glowed with anger. "So Lock tried to take the Tarkenton for himself. I shouldn't be surprised."

Victor looked over Stephanie's shoulder. "Tuney afraid to come back down?"

Stephanie frowned. "What do you mean?"

Muscles tightened at the bottom of Victor's stomach. "Tuney didn't fill you in?"

She shook her head. "I never saw Tuney. Luca and I showed up and found the grate locked at the top of the ladder. We forced it open and came in to get you."

Brooke bit her lip. "Do you think he didn't get out?"

"Oh, I think he got out, all right," Victor said.

The truth hit her like a sandbag.

Tuney got out.

And he'd left them there.

Perhaps he went to meet up with Lock.

Or the former bad cop had found the painting somewhere and decided to cash in for himself. She sensed that was what Victor was thinking. Once again, Brooke had not been able to see the treachery right in front of her nose. She hadn't liked Tuney, but she'd believed him.

Victor led them forward. "We can worry about Tuney later. Right now we've got to get Colda before he disappears."

"With the Tarkenton," Denise said grimly.

Brooke's frustrations over the past days boiled over. "I don't care if he has the painting or not. I don't care if we find the Tarkenton anyway. I just want to get Dad out of the mess he's in."

Denise's eyebrows shot up. "That painting is priceless. We can't leave it down here. If Colda gets away we might never know where he stashed it." She gestured to the filth around them and shuddered. "Your father would not agree with that decision."

"Maybe Dad is wrong, then," Brooke said, kicking aside a piece of broken pipe. "It's just a thing, not a person." Not a living, breathing Tad, or a wounded Stryker, or, she thought with a look ahead, a Victor Gage.

Denise took her around the shoulders as they pushed along. "You've been through a lot. I forgot that for a moment. I'm sorry."

The way narrowed until they moved into single file. The air was still warm, carrying the faint scent of burned wire from the explosion. They came to another dead end and a ladder, which they climbed one at a time until Brooke found herself in a utility room. The sight of painted walls after the endless expanse of concrete was a shock to her vision. "Are we out of the tunnels?"

Victor examined two sets of doors on either side. "Hard to say. Which way did Colda go? He couldn't have gotten out any other way."

Stephanie bent over and squinted at the door frame.

"This one," she said, pointing to another pawn drawn on the metal.

They tried the door but it wouldn't open. Victor kicked at it a few times, hard enough to crash against the metal with an awful din. The door gave just enough for him to push a hand through and remove the chair that was wedged against the handle on the other side. Brooke followed Victor into a bleak hallway, her eyes dazzled by the fluorescent lighting, dim though it was, and the strange feel of smooth floor underfoot.

"Where are we?" Denise said, blinking.

Victor read the sign on the utility room door. "Administration building. Lock's office is to the left."

They padded quickly across the linoleum, listening as they did so for hints that Colda was ahead of them.

Victor stopped suddenly, near an open door. Angry voices came from inside.

"It's Lock's outer office," he whispered in her ear before turning to Stephanie. "Go call Luca." She nodded and moved silently down the hallway.

Brooke finally recognized the two voices, Tuney and Dean Lock.

"You've used me from the start," Tuney barked.

"You were paid well for your trouble."

"I wasn't paid enough to lose Fran."

"Don't be absurd."

"You don't care about your missing professor."

"No, and you didn't either," Lock said, voice low

and steely. "You came for the paycheck, so my motives aren't important here."

Tuney spoke again, his voice so low Brooke almost didn't catch it. "That's where you're wrong. Something you don't know about me is that I go after the truth like a starving dog after a steak dinner. You will tell me what I want to know," Tuney said. There was the sound of a gun being cocked. "Or I'll put a bullet in your head."

TWENTY-ONE

Victor was through the door before Brooke processed what was happening. As she entered, Tuney's face and Lock's wore the same expression of surprise. Tuney kept a gun pointed at Lock in spite of their unexpected arrival.

Tuney grinned but the smile did not reach his eyes. "I see you got out okay."

"No thanks to you," Victor said.

"I finally slogged my way out of the tunnels in time to see your sister and brother on their way in. I knew they'd find you quickly."

It was probably another in his long string of lies, Brooke thought. "Or you left us there to die."

He looked at her and she thought she saw a flicker of emotion deep down in his eyes. "Think what you want."

"Why are you doing this to Lock?" Brooke said.

Tuney kept the gun steady. "You won't believe what I found walking around those idiotic tunnels." He pulled a cell phone from his pocket and tossed it to Victor. "Colda's. An old model, doesn't even text, and the professor has no idea how to delete messages. He has over a hundred on there. Took me quite a while to go through them. There's a very interesting message from the dean here."

The dean's face turned ashen. "I don't know what you're talking about."

"Play it," Tuney said, rage thrumming through his words. "Come closer so we can all enjoy."

Victor held up the phone and pressed the button.

The message was tinny but clear, the voice unmistakably Lock's.

"Send the note to Donald and tell him it was a fake. There will be an accident, a fire or flooding problem, and you'll let him know the painting was destroyed. I know a collector who would die for it. We'll split the fee. Don't talk to anyone about this." The message clicked off.

Tuney's face was a mask of disgust. "He was pressuring Colda to lie to Donald. Colda probably went on the run because he couldn't figure any other way out, poor sap. What I want to know now is, did you have Stryker keep tabs on Brooke? Worried that she might hire Victor and find your painting?"

"No," the dean said, lips nearly as white as his pale face. "I've never heard of any Stryker. Colda disappeared with the painting and that's why I hired you to find him."

"Do you believe him?" Tuney asked, looking at Brooke and Victor.

"I don't," Denise said. "I learned a long time ago that he wasn't to be trusted."

"I don't either," Tuney said. "I'm not going to be satisfied with any half-baked truth. I want to know why Fran is dead, and you're going to tell me."

Sweat rolled down Lock's face. "I don't know anything about that. Shooting me will not change my story. It's the truth."

"Put the gun down," Victor said to Tuney. "He's telling the truth. Lock wouldn't have any way of knowing Brooke would come to us, so he couldn't have sent Stryker."

Tuney hesitated and then lowered his weapon.

Lock hunched over his desk, hands pressed to his temples. "You all have no idea. That was a Tarkenton, a previously unknown work done by a master artist, the greatest of his time. How could anyone see such a thing, touch such a thing and let it out of their grasp?" His eyes were wide, the whites showing wetly in his pale face as he focused on Brooke. "It was not right that your father should have it."

"Not right?" Denise hissed. "He spent years on the trail of that painting. It was all he had left after being disgraced."

"I was disgraced, too." A bead of sweat rolled off Lock's chin and plopped onto the desk.

"You deserved to be disgraced," Denise said. "You were never worthy to be the curator of that museum."

"No," he said, spittle flying from his mouth. "That's what you should have been, cold woman that you are. You would have been right at home in a gallery of stone and glass."

Denise stepped forward and slapped him, the sound making Brooke jump. "And how could I ever hope to be a curator when I lost everything because of you?" She whirled on her heel and stalked out of the room.

Lock sank down with an expression of utter defeat, his twisted hand lying limply on his desk.

Brooke tried to sort out what she'd just experienced. "I've got to go after her."

Victor nodded. "We'll stay here in case Colda shows up."

Brooke went into the hallway but saw no sign of Denise, so she returned to Lock's office. Stephanie strode up with Luca at her side, bringing him up to speed.

Luca shook his head. "So you've got no Colda and no painting. Losing your touch, big brother? The barracuda is going to take a loss on this case?"

Victor laughed, but Brooke could see the remark had hit home. Victor was not a man who liked to lose.

She had other reasons to feel defeated. Colda hadn't been able to shed any light on the long-ago theft and it seemed he never would. She sank into a chair and watched Luca and Victor prowl the space, opening the door and checking again the inner office where they had met with the dean before. The space was empty and cold, the same rich carpet and solitary piano.

Stephanie clicked off the phone. "Cops are waiting outside. They've got a few questions for us. The university president is with them, and he's not in a good mood from what I gather."

Brooke struggled to her feet and they made their way outside and found two police vehicles waiting. Tuney escorted Lock firmly by the arm. "I'm sure the president will want to have a word with you, Dean Lock."

Brooke was asked by Detective Paulson to sit on the administration-building steps while he proceeded to debrief Victor, who recited in weary detail everything that had transpired. It took him quite a while, but the bottom line didn't change—no Colda, no treasure.

Her heart sank. No hope for her father.

The sun sank into the horizon and fingers of fog began to twine themselves through the campus in and amongst the buildings. Detective Paulson had only begun to listen to Brooke's version of the events when he got a call on his radio.

"You'll need to come down to the station so we can continue this. I'll meet you there as soon as I can."

She nodded.

Paulson leveled a stern glance at her. "I've got two more units coming to search for Colda, so don't get any ideas about going back into those tunnels."

Even the thought of heading underground made

Brooke shudder. "I understand. I'll just pack my things and meet you at the station."

Victor walked her back to the dorm. After a few paces he put his arm around her and she relaxed into his touch, fatigue suddenly overwhelming her.

"I'm sorry we didn't find your Tarkenton."

She was too tired to do anything but nod. The fog lay thick over the campus, stars beginning to twinkle in the dark patches between the eerie tendrils. "You're going back tonight."

It wasn't a question, more a statement.

He cleared his throat. "I guess so. I think the police are going to lock this place down. I thought maybe—" he looked down "—maybe we could go somewhere after you talk to the police."

His tone mystified her. "Go somewhere and do what?"

"Just talk. I…I want to tell you some things."

She saw the guilt in his face. He felt bad that he hadn't been able to find the painting. The treasure seeker had failed. What was more, she thought she could detect pity, pity for the girl that would return to a father about to be arrested and a brother whom she did not have the means to bring home again. Tears welled up. "It's better if we just say our goodbyes. I've got to get to the airport as soon as possible." *Before they have enough evidence to put my father away.*

Victor raised a hand and she thought he was going to cup her cheek.

He let it fall away and for a moment the ache inside er was overwhelming. She hurried her pace until ley came to the dorm. The lights were on when they ntered. Stephanie was already nearly packed up.

Brooke frowned. "I thought my aunt would be ack here."

Stephanie shook her head. "Haven't seen her."

"She wouldn't have left without her things," Brooke said, fingering her aunt's jacket. A feeling of read rose inside her like rising floodwaters. Slowly he looked to Victor. "Did you see her at all when we vere talking to the police?"

He shook his head, face grave. "No. Second time he's missing."

Brooke waited only a moment before she ran back ut into the night.

Victor exchanged a look with Stephanie as she rabbed her jacket. "I thought we were done."

"I did, too," Victor said, jogging down the hall.

Luca met them on the threshold. "Who are we fter now?" he said, falling in behind.

Victor didn't answer, emerging into the darkness ist in time to see Brooke darting across the grounds ack toward the building where Tuney had recently eld Lock at gunpoint. He overtook her after a hard print. "Where are you going?"

"I saw a light. At least I thought I saw one, in the rindow of the dean's office."

He stopped her. "Are you sure?"

"No."

He was unsure, too, but not about what she'd seen. Something had changed inside him down in the tunnels and he desperately wanted to tell her, but now was not the time. He had the despondent feeling that there never would be the right time. She would return to her father. He would go back to treasure hunting. Whatever he'd felt or imagined would slide back into the darkness. He swallowed back the feeling.

"We're going, too," he said as Luca and Stephanie joined them.

"And I thought the fun was over," Luca said. "Are we going to do some breaking and entering?"

"Just looking around. If there's anything out of place, we go to the cops," Victor said.

"Stick-in-the-mud," Luca said with a grin.

They skirted the building and made it around to the farside, where Lock's office faced the courtyard. One small window was covered by a curtain. He opened his mouth to suggest they search another area when Brooke gasped. "There," she whispered, grabbing his arm.

He saw it, too, the quick flash of light where there shouldn't be any, visible for only a second behind the curtain.

Stephanie pointed to the side of the building. "Luca and I will take the front in case it's Colda and he makes a run for it."

He understood. "Okay. We've got the back." He took Brooke's hand and they jogged around to the rear. They found the door locked with a padlock. He narrowly avoided the urge to kick the door.

Brooke tugged at his arm as he looked for another way in. "The window," she whispered, pointing.

The window in the next office over was slightly ajar. He pushed at it, easing it as far as he could before giving Brooke a boost and hauling himself over the sill. They dropped down onto plush carpet, the room completely dark and silent.

Moving quietly, he raced to the door, Brooke right behind him. Easing it open they were now in the hallway just outside Lock's office. Luca and Stephanie had not arrived yet. From inside Lock's office they heard a soft clang.

Victor crouched low and turned the knob. The door opened and they could see into the outer reception area. Quiet and empty.

The intruder was in the rear, in Lock's personal chambers.

He knew it would do no good to tell Brooke to wait until he checked it out, so he endeavored to keep her behind him as he crept to the second door. It was ajar but he could not make out any movement inside. He straightened slowly and ran his fingers up the wall near the door frame, searching for the light switch.

A soft scraping sound made him freeze. Someone was in the office, not four feet away.

The soft shush of feet across the carpet.

His nerves fired.

The squeak of an office chair.

Victor realized he could wait no longer. He found
the switch and flipped it on.

The room sprang into view and he blinked against
the sudden brilliance.

The intruder did, too. Denise shaded her face with
her hand from her seat in Lock's office chair.

Brooke gasped. "What…?"

Denise's surprise gave way to consternation. She
put a finger to her lips. They heard the scratching
noise coming from somewhere in the walls. Before
he could stop her, Denise ran to the wall and turned
off the light again.

"Aunt Denise," Brooke whispered. "What is going
on here?"

There was just enough moonlight shining through
the open drapes in the outer office for him to see her
response. She merely shook her head, bits of debris
from their tunnel adventure still caught in her hair.
Victor was about to turn the lights on again and force
Denise to come clean when the panel covering the
air duct on the ceiling suddenly came loose. A set of
feet shimmied down through the space, followed by
legs in dirty trousers.

When the feet hit the floor, Brooke turned on the
light again and Leo Colda covered his eyes and collapsed to the carpet, hands clapped over his eyes.

"How did you know he'd come back here?" Brooke
said, her own eyes wide with surprise.

Denise folded her arms. "I was upset, after hearing Lock's confession. I walked the halls of this

building for a while and I heard him, up there, in the ductwork." She glared at Colda. "I knew he would have to wait until night before he would make his move. I went into the next office to wait for Colda." She moved closer. "You shouldn't have taken Donald's painting. He trusted you, Leo. Now where is it?"

He didn't answer, face white, mouth open.

She kicked his foot. "I said where is it?"

Brooke caught her arm. "Don't. He's scared."

"Scared?" Denise snorted. "We were scared, too, chasing after you through those tunnels. Now, where is it?"

Colda found his voice. "I'll never give it to you."

"Yes, you will," Denise said. "We're not letting you out of this room until you tell us where it is."

Victor noticed a cruel note in Denise's voice that he hadn't heard before.

"Professor Colda, Dean Lock has been forced to tell the truth, that he tried to get you to lie about the painting. He worked with Stryker, the young man who was shot, to find you, but now they're both out of the picture, so to speak."

Colda shook his head. "No. It's not safe."

"Yes, it is," Brooke said, soothingly, kneeling next to him. "Just, please, tell us why you left a note confessing to the museum theft. Did you help Lock with the burglary all those years ago and leave my father to take the blame?"

Colda shook his head violently. Slowly he pointed a shaking finger. "She did."

Victor and Brooke turned to stare at Denise.

"I saw her with the kid," Colda said, "the day Donald came to meet me. She thought no one saw them talking and plotting together but I did. When I called later to tell Donald his cousin was after the Tarkenton, she answered so I hung up quick. Made plans to go see him myself."

"He's crazy," she said. "Now, where's the Tarkenton?"

Colda's lips trembled. "She and the kid drove me off the road. She tried to force me to tell her where I'd hidden the Tarkenton. She pushed me and I fell and hit my head on the car. I woke up in the water, I nearly drowned. When you told me about the 'confession' note I supposedly sent to the police, I knew it was her."

Denise looked coldly at the professor. "I thought you were dead. It would have been better if you were. Then Donald would be cleared and Stryker would have eventually found the painting." Her voice became thoughtful. "I was so sure we would find it."

Colda clasped and unclasped his hands, turning desperate eyes on Brooke. "I tried to warn you. I left the pawn on your pillow."

Victor could not believe what he was hearing. Brooke clasped her aunt's arm. "Tell me he's lying."

She studied Brooke for a long moment before she sighed. "I never meant for your father to be blamed, Brooke. I arranged the burglary using your father's codes, but I counted on Lock taking the fall. He was the head curator." She gripped Brooke's hand. "Really, I never meant to hurt your father. Colda's suicide note should have cleared him."

Vaguely Victor became aware of a slight movement in the outer office. Luca and Stephanie. He wanted to keep Denise talking before anything could distract her from telling the whole truth. "We didn't miss the authentication paper in Colda's place, did we? You planted that to keep me on the case."

"Lock wouldn't have let us back into the tunnels without you." Denise shook her head. "It was too good to be true, when your father found that Tarkenton. Imagine how I felt when I discovered he'd sent it away for appraisal without my consent. A priceless treasure like that, shipped off to a worm like Colda after the years I'd spent helping Donald."

Brooke's expression was stark. "You ruined my father, and you left Colda for dead."

"What about Fran?" Victor said.

"Who?"

"The woman killed in my office."

Denise waved a hand. "That was an accident. I didn't want anyone else looking for that painting so I paid Stryker to scare you, Brooke. I knew he was an idiot when I met him in San Francisco, but he was desperate for the money. I didn't dream he would actually shoot someone."

Victor's jaw tightened. "He killed two people. My

wife died outside the museum when Stryker was getting away with the sketches."

Denise shook her head. "That was an accident, too."

An accident for which he'd blamed the wrong man. He looked to Brooke, wishing he could whisk her away from this scene. Her world was being turned upside down one more time. The pain and betrayal showed in the agony on her face.

He took one step toward her when Denise turned the tables, pulling a gun from her pocket and circling behind Colda. "I found this in the tunnels, so I took if for safety's sake. I'm sorry. I really am."

TWENTY-TWO

Brooke felt as though she was trapped in a nightmare. "I thought I knew you."

Denise pressed the gun to Colda's temple. "Knew me? You knew me as the washed-up aunt who never made anything of herself. I had dreams, Brooke. Like you I had dreams of becoming something. I lost out on college, lost my baby. It was all taken from me, so I tried to take some of it back."

"By stealing," Victor snapped. "You ruined Brooke's father."

Denise's jaw tightened. "I told you. Lock was supposed to take the blame for that, not Donald. None of that is important. All that matters now is the Tarkenton."

Brooke hated the look of terror on Colda's face. Tears leaked out from his eyes.

"Please, stop," Brooke begged. "Don't hurt him."

"I won't. If he tells me where the Tarkenton is. He came back here to the office for a reason."

Colda got to his feet, knees shaking visibly. "I can't," he said piteously.

"Oh, yes, you can," Denise said, pushing him with the gun. She followed behind Colda while keeping an eye on Victor and Brooke.

Out of the corner of her eye she could see Victor tense, and she felt his desire to act.

Don't, Victor.

The thought of him getting shot was too much for her distressed mind.

Colda shuffled to the corner of the office. With a desperate glance at Brooke and Victor, he opened the top lid of the piano, reached in and pulled out a thin, rectangular case.

Denise laughed. "Of course Lock would never find it there. He can't play a note anymore. How ironic."

Victor let out a breath. "So all this time, it was right here. It never was in the tunnels at all."

"It was at first," Colda said. "But I didn't dare keep it there long. The conditions might have damaged it."

Brooke's mind boggled at the lunacy of it all. Lives risked, ended and thrown away because of a painting, a pretty lady made of pencil and paint.

"Put it on the desk," Denise commanded. "And open it."

With trembling fingers, Colda opened the latches on the case and flipped open the lid. They all took a step forward and Brooke saw that this time, the treasure had been found.

The Contemplative Lady gazed out her window, wistful and lovely, apparently undamaged by her time hidden in the piano.

Denise's gaze was rapt as she stared at it. "So beautiful," she breathed.

Victor edged around the side, but she snapped out of her reverie. "No heroics, Mr. Gage."

Brooke took the opportunity to snatch the painting out of the box.

Both Denise and Colda gasped.

She held it taut, over the top of a chair.

"What are you doing?" Denise gasped. "Be careful."

"You're going to put the gun down," she heard herself say, "or I'm going to put the chair right through the middle of the painting."

Denise's eyes widened, then narrowed. She shifted the gun away from Colda and right toward Victor's heart. "Brooke, you know what you're holding there. You know your family's future is in that painting."

Tears started in her eyes and ran down her face. The words of Matthew 6:21 echoed in her memory. Treasures were not to be found in the things of the world.

For where your treasure is, there will your heart be also. She knew her aunt's heart was entwined in the Tarkenton, in the forbidden sketches she'd hidden away. But where was Brooke's heart? At the moment Denise aimed the gun at Victor, Brooke knew.

Her heart belonged to Victor Gage.

Even though he would never claim it.

Denise gripped the gun tighter and Brooke readied herself to ruin her father's dream. She raised the painting. Victor, mouth closed in a thin line, eyes burning with intensity, spun around so quickly she almost didn't see it. His elbow connected with Denise's ribs. She grunted and stumbled back just as Luca and Stephanie hurtled through the door.

Luca tackled Denise before she could recover her footing. She went down.

Brooke realized she'd been stopped in her effort to ruin the painting. Someone held her arm. She looked up to find Stephanie gently prying her fingers off the frame. Her eyes were gentle. "No need to do that now, Brooke. It's all over, honey."

Brooke relinquished her hold on the Tarkenton and stepped back.

It's all over.

The words brought no comfort. Victor and Luca were pulling Denise to her feet and Colda sat down at the desk, staring at the painting lovingly, as if it were a perfect infant.

Feeling suddenly sick and filled with despair, Brooke ran out of the office. She found herself in the grassy courtyard, heedless of the rain that had begun to fall.

She'd gotten all that she wanted. Her father would be cleared. He would have his Tarkenton. She could go home to Tad and leave San Francisco buried in the fog forever. But grief welled up inside at the thought of all she had lost. Her aunt, her blind trust.

And her heart.

She sank to her knees and gave her tears to God until she found Victor crouched next to her.

"I'm sorry," he said.

She could not answer.

He reached a hand out to her but stopped before he made contact. "Brooke, I blamed your father. I accused an innocent man and I'm sorry. I am going to offer my apologies in person to him."

It didn't seem to matter anymore. The words rolled off her like the falling rain.

He hesitated. "Luca called the police. They'll be here in a minute."

She forced herself to answer. "I…I just need some time. To pray."

He sank to his knees on the grass next to her and took her hand gently in his. "I don't know how to pray, but I'll stay with you, if you'll let me."

She squeezed his hand and poured out her anguish into the night.

Victor answered the questions again, settled into his uncomfortable seat at the police station. He caught sight of Brooke, her face pallid, eyes shadowed with fatigue. When Detective Paulson finally released them both, Victor took Brooke's arm. She felt small and lifeless in his grasp. "It's late. I'll take you to Stephanie's for the night. We can talk in the morning."

She didn't respond as he led her out through the waiting area. Tuney was there, gruff and unkempt, eating from a box of animal crackers. He got to his feet. "Hey, Doc. Heard you found your treasure after all," he said, eyeing Brooke.

"Yeah. And how is it that you're still a free man after threatening Dean Lock at gunpoint?"

Tuney grinned. "The dean is still hoping to keep his story out of the public eye, so he didn't press charges. At the least, the guy's gonna lose his job for sure." He sobered and reached out a hand to Victor. "I want to thank you. Fran deserved to have her killer caught."

They shook hands. "I didn't do much. If Colda hadn't come back for the Tarkenton, we might never have known Denise was behind everything." Victor shot a look at Brooke, who had come alive at the mention of Fran's name.

She suddenly wrapped her arms around the startled Tuney. "I'm sorry my aunt was behind Fran's death. I'm so, so sorry."

Tuney's face softened and he patted her gruffly on the back. "Not your fault, kiddo. Like I said, family can get you into all kinds of trouble."

She pulled away, face wet with tears, and he gave her another awkward pat. "You're a good girl. If you ever need help from a crotchety old geezer, let me know. Good luck." He walked out of the station.

Stephanie took Brooke around the shoulders and led her away. Victor watched them until Luca appeared at his side.

"Satisfied with the case?" Luca said.

Victor shrugged. "Why wouldn't I be? Treasure Seekers has another tally in the win column. Treasure found, bad folks in jail. Good PR."

Luca was looking at him strangely. "That's it, then? On to the next case?"

"What more is there?" Brooke was so far away now he could barely see her. So far away. He could still feel her cold hand in his as they sat together on the grass. He'd accused her father. He'd staked four years of life on the need for revenge. Now it had all changed and he felt as though he was in a rudderless boat in a storm-tossed ocean.

The only light in his life had been Brooke Ramsey.

And now, as he strained the darkness to find her, he could not.

He didn't sleep; the apartment walls closed in on him like the endless tunnels they'd traversed. Finally, in the bitter hours of the night before the sun rose, he put on his shoes and ran until the fog collected on his hair and his muscles screamed their displeasure. When he could maintain the pace no longer, he walked.

Hours later he did not realize where he'd headed until he found himself wandering the streets of San Francisco's Valencia corridor at five o'clock in the morning. Thoughts chased themselves around in his head, snatches of conversation with Brooke, the sunshine that seemed trapped in her heart and spirit, her smile that had somehow embedded itself inside him.

Victor was not a sentimental man, not a spiritual or spontaneous man. He was someone who looked for answers and found them, allowed himself to be ruled by reason and research, yet he could not explain why he found himself on the doormat of his sister's condo on Clinton Park as the sky showed the first blush of morning. He stared at the bell, feeling almost as surprised as Brooke appeared to be when she opened the door to discover him there, sweaty and disheveled. He noted the suitcase in her hand.

"Good morning," she said, giving him a faint version of the smile that went to the core of him. "I was just on my way to the airport. Luca's driving me."

Victor nodded. "How is your father?"

Her smile dimmed. "I reached him by phone but…"

"It would be better to try to explain about your aunt in person." He saw the sadness rise up in her eyes. "How are you doing with everything?"

"I'm going to have a hard time making sense of it. All the years I believed she was something entirely different than what she turned out to be. I was too trusting. Dumb."

"No. You loved her. That's not dumb."

She didn't respond at first. "I told him about the Tarkenton, but I'm not sure he understood fully. It may be years before it can be authenticated properly. I'm going to suggest to my father that we donate it to the museum." She sighed. "I just want my father's name credited as the one who found it."

He wasn't surprised at her decision. "What will you do about your father and Tad?"

"I'm not sure yet. Somehow I'll figure it out."

"I'd like to help," he blurted out so abruptly it made her jump.

"What?"

"I'd like to help you get your father situated with a good team of doctors I know. Help you find a good in-home nurse for Tad. We can sell your story to some magazines and TV if you feel like you can share it."

A thoughtful expression crossed her face. "That would be painful, but it would allow me to clear my father in the public eye."

"And I would like to help in the meantime. Get Tad back home until things come together."

She looked at him closely, a section of freshly washed hair falling across her cheek. "I appreciate what you've done for me, Victor. And I know you feel bad about my father, but I don't hold a grudge. I really don't. There's no need for you to do that."

"Yes, there is."

"What reason?"

He felt a mixture of terror and elation bubble inside him. "Something happened to me."

She put down her suitcase. "Do you want to sit down? You look flushed."

"No, no." He began to pace in tight circles as he spoke, willing himself to say the things that were fighting to stay inside. "Brooke, meeting you has changed me. In the years after Jennifer died I felt like my insides turned to stone, and that was just fine by me. It is my natural tendency to be aloof and judgmental and maybe even ruthless."

"Sea Tiger." A ghost of a smile danced on her mouth before she pressed her lips together and clasped her arms around her front. "What are you saying, Victor?"

"I'm saying that for some reason that I don't understand, I no longer feel angry inside." He paced faster. "How can I explain it?" With frantic fingers he fished out his wallet and pulled out the scrap of paper with Pearson, Jackney and Rivera's names. "Here."

She took it, a look of wonder on her face. "Why are you giving this to me?"

"Because finally I think I can let them go, because I've accepted that I'm not going to get the answer and even if I did, it wouldn't change anything. I don't understand it myself. Your faith, your trust that God is in charge, I don't comprehend it or accept it, but I think…"

She reached out and took his offered hand in hers. "Tell me."

"I think I'm open to listening." He wasn't sure he'd really managed to say the words until he saw her smile, a dazzling full-lipped grin that lifted his spirits and made him dizzy.

"I'm so glad," she said.

He pulled her close. "Brooke, there's something else." His hands smoothed her copper hair, soaking in the satiny glide of it. Her eyes were so wide, so blue, he felt as though he'd dived into them. "I think...I'm falling in love with you." It was more than a thought. Standing in front of him was the woman he would marry in time. He was dead certain.

She started, but he would not let her pull away.

His words tumbled on in a rush. "I haven't known you long and this is probably scaring you because it scares me, but the fact is, I can't get you out of my mind or my heart and nothing in my life will make any sense if you're not in it."

She reached out a hand and stroked his cheek. "Oh, Victor," she breathed. "I can't believe you're saying this."

"I can't either, but if I don't I know I'm going to regret it for the rest of my life."

Her eyes clouded. "But if my father had been guilty..."

"If your father had been guilty, I would feel exactly the same about you. I knew it the moment I nearly lost you in the flood. I didn't want to believe that it was love, especially not for you."

She looked down and he reached a finger under her chin and gently brought her gaze to his.

"I'm not asking you to give up anything to fit me into your life. I just want to know that you might feel the same way someday. I have to know if there's the possibility of a future with you."

She began to cry.

"Please, Brooke," he said, pressing kisses onto her

tear-streaked face. "Please, tell me we can build a life together. Just try, that's all I'm asking."

"But I might…" She began to shudder.

"You might what?"

"I might…have the disease my father has." It came out a whisper, and in it he heard the fear that she'd kept inside for so long.

"It doesn't matter."

"Yes, it does," she said, pulling away and turning from him. "My mind could get jumbled like my father's. It's a genetic flaw. Maybe someday—" she began to cry in earnest "—maybe someday I won't even know who you are."

He could feel the pain radiating out of her and he clasped her hand as if he could siphon some of it away. "You'll always know who I am."

"How do you know that?"

He cocked his head. "Someone once told me that faith is believing when you can see all around you the reasons to doubt."

She wiped her face with her sleeve. "That was some pretty smart stuff."

"From a pretty smart lady."

She looked away. "I've booked a flight."

"Cancel it," he said, grabbing her hand.

"I have to find a job."

He would not let her pull away. "I'll help."

She shook her head. "The press will hound my family."

"I'll scare them off," he said, drawing her closer

until he pulled her to his chest, pressing his lips to her cheek, her forehead, her temples. "Tell me you could love me."

She sighed, a deep ragged sound. "I'll tell you the truth, Victor."

He saw a sparkle of tears in her eyes and his heart pounded against his ribs.

"The truth is," she said, blue eyes luminous, "I already do."

Joy surged inside him at a level he'd never thought possible as he molded his mouth to hers. Her love traveled through his lips into his soul, lighting a flame there that he knew he would treasure until his dying day.

A sound from the window drew their attention.

Luca and Stephanie crowded into the open second-floor window, smiling.

"About time," Luca said. "Big brother's finally found his treasure."

"Yes, he has," Victor said with a laugh, pulling Brooke to him for another kiss.

* * * * *

Dear Reader,

I've been a treasure seeker all my life. When I was little, I was convinced that the bits of colored glass and feathers I collected were precious and I hoarded them in secret drawers and boxes. Later, I decided frogs were the thing, and I've amassed a collection of stone, porcelain, glass and wooden frogs. I even have one made out of sand! As I've gotten older and my little children are not so little anymore, my idea of treasure has changed. Now it's the rickety hand-crafted ornaments from kindergarten and the pictures drawn with chubby crayons that I value. Each captures a moment gone by, a love memory that is as intangible as it is profound.

There are surely a lot of worldly treasures to pursue, aren't there? The new car. The bigger house, the better job, an amazing vacation. Funny how none of these treasures could replace one happy moment with my children or a fond memory of time spent with my husband, sisters or parents. Our treasures truly are the things of the heart, the people that God has blessed us with for a season, aren't they? I hope and pray that I can truly value those kinds of treasures here on earth, which are surely just a small taste of the Heavenly wealth God has in store for each and every one of us.

I am so pleased that you spent time with this book, the first of the Treasure Seekers series. I would love to hear from you via my website at www.danamentink.com. There's an address there if you prefer to correspond by letter. God bless.

Sincerely,

Dana Mentink

Questions for Discussion

1. Brooke is a person who lost her dream of becoming a dancer. Have you experienced the loss of a particular dream or aspiration? What helped you cope with the loss and move on?

2. Victor Gage is from a wealthy family. Since profit is not his primary motivation, why does he passionately pursue treasure hunting?

3. Stephanie is described as fearless. Do you know anyone who comes across that way? How did they come by such a quality?

4. Colda orders grilled cheese and tomato sandwiches and black coffee every day. What does this repetitive habit tell you about his character? What repetitive habits do you have and what do they reveal about you?

5. Tad has Fragile X Syndrome. What has your experience been with the mentally challenged? What direction can we find in the Bible to guide us in this area?

6. Victor asks Brooke if she's afraid God isn't listening. Are there times in our lives when we

feel this way? What is the antidote for spiritual silence?

7. Victor carries the names of the three patients who die without apparent cause. Why do you think he clings so tightly to those three cases? Can you draw any parallels to your own life?

8. "It's just a painting," Brooke says of the Tarkenton. What material objects do we prize above all others? What are some Biblical comments on worldly wealth?

9. Tuney has a shady past. What is your opinion of him at the end of the novel?

10. What do you think of Brooke's threat to destroy the Tarkenton? What action would you have taken in her place?

11. Victor sees the world in black and white. Do you know people who are similar? What is the strength of such a life view? The weakness?

12. What do you think will happen to Victor's faith journey after the adventure is over? What makes you think so?

13. In our society, people spend their lives pursuing various worldly riches. What things do people seek instead of Godly treasures?

14. Brooke decides to donate the Tarkenton to the museum. Would you make the same decision? Why or why not?

15. What kind of adventures lie ahead for the Treasure Seekers?

LARGER-PRINT BOOKS!

**GET 2 FREE
LARGER-PRINT NOVELS
PLUS 2 FREE
MYSTERY GIFTS**

Love Inspired®

SUSPENSE
RIVETING INSPIRATIONAL ROMANCE

Larger-print novels are now available...

LARGER-PRINT BOOKS!

GET 2 FREE
LARGER-PRINT NOVELS
PLUS 2 FREE
MYSTERY GIFTS

Love Inspired

Larger-print novels are now available...

YES! Please send me 2 FREE LARGER-PRINT Love Inspired® novels and my 2 FREE mystery gifts (gifts are worth about $10). After receiving them, if I don't wish to receive any more books, I can return the shipping statement marked "cancel". If I don't cancel, I will receive 6 brand-new novels every month and be billed just $4.99 per book in the U.S. or $5.49 per book in Canada. That's a saving of at least 23% off the cover price. It's quite a bargain! Shipping and handling is just 50¢ per book in the U.S. and 75¢ per book in Canada.* I understand that accepting the 2 free books and gifts places me under no obligation to buy anything. I can always return a shipment and cancel at any time. Even if I never buy another book, the two free books and gifts are mine to keep forever.

122/322 IDN FEG3

Name _____ (PLEASE PRINT)

Address _____ Apt. #

City _____ State/Prov. _____ Zip/Postal Code

Signature (if under 18, a parent or guardian must sign)

Mail to the **Reader Service:**
IN U.S.A.: P.O. Box 1867, Buffalo, NY 14240-1867
IN CANADA: P.O. Box 609, Fort Erie, Ontario L2A 5X3

Not valid to current subscribers to Love Inspired Larger-Print books.

Are you a current subscriber to Love Inspired books
and want to receive the larger-print edition?
Call 1-800-873-8635 or visit www.ReaderService.com.

* Terms and prices subject to change without notice. Prices do not include applicable taxes. Sales tax applicable in N.Y. Canadian residents will be charged applicable taxes. Offer not valid in Quebec. This offer is limited to one order per household. All orders subject to credit approval. Credit or debit balances in a customer's account(s) may be offset by any other outstanding balance owed by or to the customer. Please allow 4 to 6 weeks for delivery. Offer available while quantities last.

Your Privacy—The Reader Service is committed to protecting your privacy. Our Privacy Policy is available online at www.ReaderService.com or upon request from the Reader Service.

We make a portion of our mailing list available to reputable third parties that offer products we believe may interest you. If you prefer that we not exchange your name with third parties, or if you wish to clarify or modify your communication preferences, please visit us at www.ReaderService.com/consumerschoice or write to us at Reader Service Preference Service, P.O. Box 9062, Buffalo, NY 14269. Include your complete name and address.

LILP11B